DARK SKYE

Kate Leonard

CONTENTS

PROLOGUE

The Isle of Skye - home to the most spectacular scenery in the whole of Scotland, and arguably the most beautiful island in the world. Tourists flock here each year in their hundreds of thousands, inevitably pulled to this place, as if drawn by some giant hand. They come to experience the majestic mountains which rise fearsomely from the sea to the sky. They are left spellbound by the vertiginous cliffs which jut out into a turbulent sea. They are thrilled by tales of ancient clan battles which left rivers running red with blood.

Legend says this land was created by fairies and giants, and few could dispute this when viewing for the first time the weird, artfully-carved rock formations, the strange, saw-edged peaks and the thundering waterfalls. This is an island of extraordinary mystery, of magic. It twines around the soul, never letting go. It has been the inspiration for poetry and song for many generations. It instils a sense of romance, wonder - but maybe also of fear.

The towering Black Cuillins stand sentinel over the island, guarding the valleys and farms below with brooding menace. These are dangerous mountains, formed from treacherous, slippery basalt. Only the most experienced - or the most foolhardy – of climbers would dare to tackle them. The old Norse name for Skye translates as Cloud Island, and today that name is apt; the tops of these mountains are shrouded in mist, the jagged peaks disappearing into a leaden grey sky.

The Red Cuillins present a softer, kinder face. These rolling, rounded peaks are made of granite, which glows a rich, russet red in the sunshine. But today the sun is absent and the domes are dark and sinister.

At the foot of one of these mountains, on a craggy ridge of rock, sits a church. It is abandoned and derelict, a poignant reminder of a time when people lived and worshipped in this remote valley. The roof has long ago caved in and the walls are crumbling. A vine climbs up the far wall, as if striving to replace the missing roof. The gravestones struggle to hold themselves upright on the sloping bank below. The clan names etched into the stones bear witness to a time when this valley was a thriving hub of activity. Difficult to believe now. All that is long gone. The factory buildings, the workers' cottages – all gone. There are no dwellings, not one human even, to be seen for miles in any direction. All that remains is this solitary ruin.

A handful of sheep wander lazily amongst the gravestones, ripping at the grass with mindless determination. It is a strangely melancholic place, and utterly quiet except for the occasional bleating of the sheep and the cawing of a crow in a nearby yew tree. The grass is heavy with dew, and the sheep have kept it short.

The woman's body is lying along the length of a horizontal grave marker. The legs are neatly pressed together and the hands crossed over the chest. She is completely naked, her blue eyes wide open and staring sightlessly into the sky above. Her long hair has been carefully arranged to form a halo behind her head. Drops of dew have collected like shiny beads upon the surface of the shockingly white skin.

The sheep approach, heads down, munching steadily at the grass. They don't register the body. They don't pause to look. They are completely oblivious to the fact that a murder has been committed on this sacred site.

This most alluring of islands has a secret. Underneath the splendour, the majesty and the beauty, danger lurks. No-one expects it in such a place. But it hides, watches, ready to seek its next victim.

The gullible, unsuspecting tourists.
Such easy prey.

CHAPTER ONE: THE OLD MANSE

There was a light tap on the door. 'Are you decent? Ready to go down for dinner?' called Fran from the corridor.

'Oh, right, I'm almost ready. Um, hang on, d'you want to come in for a sec?'

Evie turned the lock and pulled the door open, not quite looking her sister in the eye. Fran marched in and began to look around the room. She paused in front of the tall sash window and gazed out towards the wall of dark mountains that towered over the lawns. Outlined against the window, Evie could see that Fran was wearing her customary elasticated waist trousers with a button-up shirt in mid blue, and sensible flat shoes. Evie couldn't help but smile affectionately. It was pretty much the same outfit she'd been wearing for the long drive up to Skye – and the one she wore on most occasions when they met. Her sister was completely her own person, uninterested in fashion trends and focused solely on comfort. Her only concession to adornment was a fine pair of pearl earrings that could be glimpsed under her short brown hair.

'You've got a better view than me. The mountains look amazing in this evening light. My window looks onto the walled gardens and the woods. It's nice enough, but I prefer yours!' Fran turned and examined the room. 'I see you've got the obligatory tartan carpet and stag painting! What's your en-suite like?' She poked her head round the bathroom door and gave a grunt of satisfaction. 'Same as mine.' Finally she looked across at her sister, who was running a brush through her shoulder-length dark brown hair. Immediately Fran's manner changed.

'Oh, Evie, have you been crying?'

'Oh, shit, is it obvious?' Evie looked at herself critically in the ornate mirror.

'Only to a sister. You just look a little pink-eyed, no-one else will notice. It's my fault, I'm an idiot. All that talking on the drive up – it's brought everything up to the surface again.'

'No, Fran, don't be daft. It was actually good to talk. I wanted to. There's a lot of stuff I've been bottling up; my head's a complete jumble of mixed up thoughts and emotions. I'm sure talking helps you sort yourself out. Don't worry, I'm just a bit flaked out, knackered, to be honest.'

'Do you miss Jake very much?' asked Fran, then immediately wished she'd held her tongue, as she saw fresh tears build in the corners of Evie's eyes.

'Yes, yes I do. But I've got to get used to the fact that we're finished. I don't think there's any way back. He's not going to forgive me.'

'You never know, it's still all quite fresh.' Fran was fond of her brother-in-law, and was hopeful for a reconciliation. 'But look, let's forget all about the past. We're here on Skye, we're going to learn how to paint like pros, we're going to drink too much whisky, meet fascinating new people, get wind- and weather-beaten and have a bloody good holiday. Yes?'

Evie smiled. 'Yes! Onwards and upwards.' She placed the hairbrush back on the table, put her phone in her handbag and straightened her spine. 'Let's go see if it's haggis for dinner!'

The sisters linked arms and made their way along the tartan-carpeted corridor, down the slightly creaking stairs, past the bar with its purple velvet armchairs and fringed table lamps, to the dining room.

The Old Manse Hotel was a good example of eighteenth century Highland architecture. Set back from a sweeping lawn, it featured two large bay windows which sat either side of the entrance. The walls were white and ivy crept around the tall multi-paned windows. Small conical turrets broke up the roofline. It must have been a fine residence for the minister and his family at one time – elegant but not too ostentatious, in keeping with the respect a minister of the Kirk was due. From the front, little had changed, but over the years the building had been extended; a wing had been added stretching out onto the gardens behind, and the stable block converted to provide more accommodation and meeting rooms for tourists. Inside, the décor was unashamedly Victorian baronial, with an overdose of wood panelling, antlers, and tartan fabric on cushions, curtains and floors. The effect was at once grand and cosy, like a hug from a favourite rich auntie.

The dining room was at the rear of the hotel, It was a big room, and unlike the bar with its intimate furnishings and log fire, it was starkly furnished with a dozen or so tables of different sizes and a single ceiling chandelier. It had been built in a newer extension to the hotel, and two sides consisted of wall to ceiling glass windows. The effect was dramatic. To the east the Black Cuillins rose up in a series of sharp, jagged cliffs separated by deep gullies. Mist lingered amongst the crevasses and the rocks shone a purplish black in the evening sun. To the west, the rough heather-covered hills gave way to green pastures that rolled down towards a blue-grey sea. It was breathtaking. Evie felt her spirits lift. She peeled her gaze away from the view and looked for a place to sit. Two of the tables were occupied by people they'd briefly met at the introductory drinks; these were some of the random mix of amateur artists who'd signed up, like herself and Fran, for the watercolour workshop holiday. Evie spotted the sleek and expensively dressed blonde, what was her name? It escaped her. Haley, Kayleigh? Something like that. There was the elderly woman with her tweed skirt and sweet, placid smile. And the stern-looking grey haired gentleman – George, she remembered, who had asked all the questions. Despite there being seats free, Evie didn't feel up to making conversation. Instead she gave the group a cheery wave and pulled Fran towards a table close to the window. Here they sat, drinking in the view. A young waitress came over and explained the menu of the day – steak pie or trout – and took their drinks order. Evie felt her shoulders drop back and her spine relax. This was going to be OK, she thought. Just what I need.

The drinks arrived and she clinked glasses with Fran, and took a large sip of refreshing white wine. 'Cheers!' she said, with genuine pleasure. 'Here's to a great holiday.'

'Cheers. So, what did you make of our art teacher this afternoon?' asked Fran.

'Oh, I think she'll be great! I like the programme: technical stuff in the morning, then outdoor painting in the afternoon, if the weather allows. And the subjects – sea, sky, rocks, water. I think I'm going to learn a lot.'

'And what did you think of the guy, the one who's going to drive the minivan and cart all the gear around?' asked Fran with a lift of an eyebrow. 'He's quite a dish isn't he?'

'You mean that Roddy guy? Huh! That combination of messy hair and old fisherman's sweater – which I'd swear smelt of fish! Yeah, he's irresistible!' Evie's voice was tinged with sarcasm.

'Didn't he remind you a bit of Jamie Fraser in Outlander? That auburn hair and those bulging muscles?'

'I think that's exactly the impression he was trying to make. Hamming up the 'rugged Highlander' act for us gullible sassenachs.'

'Cynic! He's probably Skye born and bread. Anyway, I'm glad we made it in time for the welcome drinks. It was all a bit touch and go with that protest blocking the bridge.'

Their car had been forced to wait for almost two hours on the mainland before crossing the slender Skye Bridge onto the island. They had waited patiently in a long queue of cars and camper vans, occasionally getting out and scanning the road ahead to see what the problem was. Several cars were hooting their horns impatiently. When the vehicles eventually started to move again and they made it onto the island, they saw a number of policemen shepherding protesters away onto the pavements. Evie was able to read the placards which were being waved angrily at the passing cars. 'No more Tourists' and 'Skye for the Locals' and 'Stop the cruise ships'.

'What do you make of all these anti-tourism protests?' asked Fran. 'You work in tourism. Do you think they've got a point? I mean, the island would be dead without tourism wouldn't it?'

'Well, yes and no. It depends, I suppose; if you work in a hotel or a restaurant, or a campsite, you need the tourists, but if you're just, I dunno, a postman or a doctor, and you can't afford a house because they're all Airbnbs, and can't get to work 'cos the roads are blocked with camper vans, then I guess you feel differently. It's all about setting limits.'

'But here on Skye? Isn't it just a craze? Aren't they jumping on the bandwagon? I mean, I've heard of the protests in Mallorca and Barcelona and Venice, and all that, but here? There's plenty of space here! You could fit a million tourists on the island and not feel crowded.'

'Yes, but I guess the trouble is everyone wants to go to the same five or six beauty spots. Anyway, I don't think you and I will be adding to the problem. We'll be quietly sketching on a deserted hillside somewhere, while all the other tourists queue up to see the Fairy Glen or whatever.'

'And do you come across any anti-tourism stuff in your job?' asked Fran.

Caught mid-swallow, Evie's snort of laughter caused her wine to dribble down her chin. 'You must be joking! I work for Visit Leeds! We're still trying to drag them in and make them stay! But some places in Yorkshire are struggling. Malham, or Whitby, Robin Hood's Bay, for example. It's all second homes and Airbnbs. Must be pretty awful if you're born there and can't afford to live there.' Evie pointed at Fran's empty glass. 'Shall we order a bottle this time? This wine's hitting the spot, I feel quite mellow now.'

But Evie's good mood was short-lived.

'Do you mind if we join you?' said an American voice just behind her. Evie looked round. A middle-aged couple in colourful leisure gear looked back at her expectantly.

'Oh, yes, sure!' she answered, 'Please do!' As the couple beamed and pulled their chairs back, Evie made a face at Fran, who managed not to laugh.

'I'm Marge and this is Brett. We're doing a whisky trail of Scotland. Brett loves his scotch. What about you? Have you just arrived?'

'Yes, I'm Fran and this is my sister Evie. We're here for the watercolour workshop.'

'Oh, how adorable! Sisters who paint! That's so clever.'

'Well, Evie's the painter in the family, but I'm hoping to learn a trick or two.'

'It's nice to meet you both,' said Brett, placing his napkin on his lap, 'We just love talking to new people. But I must say, you're both very brave coming here.'

'Brave?' said Evie, confused. Then her expression cleared. 'Oh, you mean the weather! We're not easily put off by the rain, we've got waterproof everything.'

'No, I don't mean the weather. I mean after what happened last week.' Brett's expression was sombre.

Evie and Fran looked from one American to the other, blankly. Fran shook her head, puzzled.

'You mean you haven't heard?' asked Marge.

'No, what do you mean? What happened last week?'

Marge leaned forward in her seat, put one hand flat on the table, looked around the room and continued in a loud, conspiratorial whisper: 'There was a murder. Right here, only about a mile or so from the hotel.'

'Really?' said Fran, 'God, that's terrible. I didn't hear anything on the news, did you, Evie?'

'No, nothing. But I don't often watch the news these days. It's too depressing.'

'It's not a pleasant thing to talk about over dinner, but I think we'd better tell you what we know, though,' said Brett. 'It might not be safe for you girls walking about alone, you know. They still haven't found out who did it.'

Evie didn't want to know any more. Her little bubble of contentment had been too short-lived and she was annoyed. She was about to say so, but there was no stopping Marge. With a touch of vicarious glee in her voice, she recounted the story.

'It was a young French woman, an influencer, or an Instagrammer, or whatever they're called. A tourist anyway. She was found, stark naked apparently, lying on top of a tombstone in a churchyard just over the hill from here.' She pointed vaguely towards the mountains. 'She'd been strangled. The police came to the hotel and asked everyone if they'd seen anything suspicious. It was horrifying.' She gave a little shiver, but Evie had a suspicion that Marge had in fact enjoyed every minute of the drama.

'You mustn't let it spoil your holiday', said Brett, kindly, 'but do be careful where you go and who you go with, until they find the killer.'

'Yes, we will, thanks,' said Fran. Then, eager to change the subject, she said brightly 'So whereabouts are you two from? That's an American accent, right?'

The rest of the meal passed in a flurry of inconsequential small-talk. They commented on the food, the glorious views, and the Americans explained their itinerary in some detail. When they'd finished eating, Brett asked if they'd care to join them at the bar for a nightcap, but Evie made apologies for them both, saying they were tired from the journey and needed an early night.

'Bloody hell,' said Fran as they walked upstairs to their rooms, 'That's the last thing we need, a murder! I'd rather not have known that!'

'I know, it's awful. That poor girl. But we'll be all right, we'll be in a large group nearly all the time. Let's not let it spoil things.'

'No, agreed. Well, this is me.' Fran searched in her bag for her room key. 'Give me a knock when you're ready tomorrow and we'll go down to breakfast together. Not too early please!' she gave her sister a brief hug, then disappeared into her room.

Evie was shattered. She undressed and lay on the bed in her own room, closed her eyes and attempted to empty her head of all thoughts. She could hear a lone owl hooting in the distance. It was a pleasant sound, soothing.

Just as she was drifting off to sleep, an image came into her head. At first hazy, the image suddenly jumped into clear and bright focus. Eyes still closed, Evie saw with perfect clarity a crumbling stone wall, it's apex pointing skywards and its window a black slit of darker stone. Tufts of grass grew out from between the rough stone blocks and luxuriant ivy climbed upwards. Beyond the wall were the dark green limbs of a stunted yew tree, illuminated from behind by a pale crescent moon. And in the middle ground, spaced out randomly on the grassy hillocks were the weathered tombstones, some rounded, some in the form of Celtic crosses, slanting drunkenly in every direction.

The body was lying in the foreground, arranged with symmetrical precision on top of a long, flat grave marker. It was shockingly naked. The skin was white and pearled with tiny drops of dew. The feet were neatly placed together, the toenails painted a vivid red in contrast to the alabaster skin. The girl's arms were crossed over each other, hiding the breasts. Her head was tilted back, as if the sightless eyes were staring up at the sky. Evie could see the bruising around the slender neck. The girl's blonde hair had been carefully arranged in a fan shape behind her head. Evie could smell the sweet odour of damp grass. She could feel that the girl's skin was as cold as marble. She could hear the wind sighing through the limbs of the twisted tree. She could even see the reflection of the moon in the drops of dew on the body. She tried to persuade herself that this was just a trick of an overactive imagination, that her brain had invented and elaborated the scene based on Marge's brief description, but in her heart she knew it was more than that. This was the crime scene in all its brilliant, vivid detail.

'Oh God,' she moaned, 'not again! Not now!'

She had come to hate these visions that interrupted her life with alarming frequency. Some were banal – a splash of rain falling on puddles, telling her to take her umbrella. Some were reassuring – her parents sitting in their garden drinking tea when she'd failed to reach them on the phone. Some were useful – a quick flash of a police car behind a hedge, telling her not to risk a third drink at her friend's house. In general she trusted these 'flashes'. She'd had them all her life. But in the last year they'd become a curse. They were the reason why Jake had … no, she mustn't think about Jake. But why this one, why now? Why was she seeing details of a past event? Was it a warning? Was she supposed to do something?

It was all too much. She'd think about it later. She took deep breaths, holding the air in her lungs, then expelling it slowly, forcing her heart rate to slow. She imagined that her limbs were attached to lead weights, that her head was heavy as a cannonball, and let her body sink back into the soft mattress. Gradually her exhaustion took over and she fell into a welcome, dreamless sleep.

CHAPTER TWO: THE FLASHES

Evie had always felt she was a lucky child. Things just seemed to work out for her. The world turned in her favour without her having to make very much effort. Sometimes she thought she had a guardian angel, smoothing the way for her. She knew things without knowing how she knew them. The phone would ring in the house, for example, and she'd say 'It's Granny!' Her mum would answer 'Yes, it could be, let's see.' And it would be Granny. She just knew.

Little things. Walking home from primary school with her older sister Fran one day, Fran had asked her:

'Do you want to go to the shop and get some sweets? I've got a bit of pocket money.' She was that kind of older sister.

'No, you don't need to bother,' Evie had replied. 'Mum's made a chocolate cake.'

'How d'you know?

'I've seen it!

'No you haven't, you daft idiot.'

'I have, in my head. It's got smarties on it.'

'You're a freak, do you know that?' Fran had laughed, bashing her none too gently on the arm. But the chocolate cake would be there on the kitchen table, waiting for them. With smarties.

Sometimes Evie felt she could make things happen. When she was ten, she was invited to her friend Harriet's birthday party. It was to be an ice-skating party. Evie couldn't skate. She knew she'd spend the entire time clinging to the edge of the rink with her feet sliding under her like a newborn calf. She didn't want to go, but she didn't worry about it. Her guardian angel would sort it. It wasn't a vision, it was more a feeling of calm certainty. And, sure enough, Harriet caught chicken pox and cancelled the party. Evie didn't feel particularly guilty about Harriet, it was just the way things were.

As she got older, she became aware that she had a gift that other people didn't have. She called it 'the flashes'. The family teased her about it: 'Evie, what's on the GCSE history paper?' Fran would ask, or 'Evie, why's your dad so late? Is he on his way home?' But Evie didn't have any control over the flashes, they came when they wanted, and mostly just for things that concerned herself.

When she started secondary school, Fran had taken her aside and warned her: 'Evie, don't tell people about the flashes. They'll think you're a weirdo. I mean, you are a weirdo, but not everyone needs to know that. Just keep it to yourself.' So she was careful. When her best friend Louise had phoned, panicking about the maths test the next day, she hadn't told her not to worry, there was going to be a fire drill that morning and maths would be cancelled.

Sometimes the flashes took a more sinister turn. When she was eighteen she took a year out to be an au pair for a Swiss family. She loved it, and was included almost as one of the family. Over the winter holidays, the family rented a chalet in the mountains to ski. Evie happily looked after the children, taking them to their ski lessons and picking them up afterwards, giving them snacks in the chalet until their parents returned. But then a couple had come to stay in the chalet: Henri and Bernadette. Henri was kind and talked to her as an equal, but Bernadette was imperious, condescending and snobbish. She treated Evie like the hired help, which, in a way, she was, and Evie hated her. One evening, after Bernadette had thrust a pile of washing into her hands and told her she needed it for the next day, Evie felt a little stirring of something inside her, a hint of power, of possibility. She didn't have to put up with this woman, she could make something happen. She went to bed with a feeling of satisfaction. The next day Bernadette broke her femur on a red run, was taken to hospital and Evie never saw her again. Had she really made that happen? Was it just a coincidence? Whatever the answer, the chalet felt a lot nicer for the rest of the holiday.

Evie sailed through the university years in a glow of confidence and positivity. The flashes became much rarer as she approached her twenties, but still she felt, a little smugly, that some 'guardian angel' was guiding her way through life, navigating a sure path around the dangers that others faced. Life was good. She made great friends, had a couple of decent boyfriends, and finished with a two-one degree in geography, without having to break much of a sweat.

And then there was Jake. Evie was twenty-five years old, and had been working for a year as a tourism officer for Leeds City Council when she met him. She loved her job and liked the city, but she was a bit lonely in Leeds, with most of her friends having moved away from Yorkshire, and Fran working as an accountant for a multinational in London. She was surprised and happy to be invited to the evening do of a colleague's wedding one weekend. She made a special effort, buying a new, figure-hugging blue dress and sweeping up her brown hair into a messy chignon. But when the evening arrived she found herself tongue-tied, unable to instigate conversations with the room full of strangers. And then she saw him. He was standing at the bar, waiting for the barman to fill up some pint glasses. He had dark blonde hair, round glasses and a strong chin covered in stubble. He was staring, rather morosely, into a pint glass. And Evie knew, with absolute certainty, that this was the man she was going to marry. She felt a rush of excitement, relief and anticipation as she walked over and introduced herself.

'Hello, I'm Evie.'

'Hi. Jake. How are you doing?'

'OK. Well, not bad considering I don't know a soul here apart from the bride, and she's a bit busy being bridal. What about you? Having fun?'

'Well, I was doing fine until I realised the free bar's over, and this round's going to cost me a bloody fortune. The prices are a joke! Oh, um, can I get you one?'

Evie laughed. 'No, you're all right. I don't want to bankrupt you. So, classic wedding question, are you a friend of the bride or groom?'

'Of Becca. She's my cousin actually, I've known her all my life. But between you and me, I don't think much of the bloke she's marrying. She's changed since she met him. She used to be a right laugh, and now she seems sort of diminished. Shit, I'm waffling. Must be a bit drunk. You might be the guy's sister for all I know. You're not, are you?'

'Yeah. I am,' said Evie, slowly. 'How did you guess?' She kept a straight face and watched the man pale.

'Shit, I'm sorry, I'm… Ah, you're joking.' He slapped himself on the forehead. 'Course, you said you only knew the bride. Duh!'

She laughed. 'No, I work with Becca at the council. She's great.'

Evie couldn't get over Jake's eyes. They were the colour of horse chestnuts, with a darker chocolate-brown rim, slightly magnified by his wire-framed glasses. I know you, she thought, you're him, you're the one. She watched him as he gathered his pints together on a tray and fished in his pocket for his wallet. He had beautiful hands too, strong. Boldly, she asked him:

'So when you've dumped your pints with your friends, do you fancy a dance?'

Jake paused and gave her a long, searching look. 'I would absolutely love to, Evie. But my girlfriend is sat on that table over there. I think she might give me a bollocking.'

Evie blushed scarlet and stuttered 'Oh, I'm sorry, I didn't think. I mean, shit, um…'

Jake stopped her with a gesture. 'Shh. Don't worry about it.' He leant down and kissed her on the cheek. Then turned back to his tray of drinks. 'See you around, Evie from the council.' And with that he was gone.

Four months later, when Evie was going out with a perfectly nice but slightly unexciting housing officer, she got a phone call.

'Hello, I don't know if you remember me...' The voice was hesitant, but she recognised it instantly. That lovely, warm Yorkshire accent. 'It's Jake. We met briefly at Becca's wedding. I'm the mug who turned down a dance with you. I got Becca to give me your phone number, I hope that's OK?'

'Um, yeah, fine! I remember. You were complaining about the price of the drinks.'

'Yeah, I'm still paying off my overdraft! So, um, I was wondering if you wanted to go out for a drink sometime?'

'I think I remember that you have a girlfriend?'

'We split up. She went back to Cardiff, where she's from. Long story, but, anyway, how about that drink?'

They arranged to meet at a Georgian style gastro-pub on the outskirts of Leeds. When Evie arrived she knew instinctively that he'd be sitting outside at one of the wooden tables, so she got herself a glass of wine and made her way through the pub towards the garden, checking her appearance in the wall mirror as she did. She looked good, she decided. Jeans, stripey t-shirt, trainers, and minimal make-up – just a touch of mascara and pink lipstick. She'd had her dark brown hair cut that morning, so it fell in light waves around her shoulders. She stopped to peer through the glass in the door panel and saw him immediately. He looked even more attractive than she remembered, in his dark blue jumper and ordinary jeans, his dirty blonde hair falling into his eyes as he took a swig from his pint glass. There was nothing particularly outstanding about him, she realised, but he looked relaxed, comfortable in his own skin, and Evie felt a sense of homecoming as she walked towards him. He stood up as she approached and kissed her on the cheek. He smelt good, masculine. She liked the way his stubble lightly grazed her skin. She liked his round glasses. She liked everything about him. And straight away the talk flowed easily. They had seen the same films, had read the same thrillers and had been to some of the same gigs. But more than that, she realised that he was a genuinely decent person; he was kind, funny and interested in her opinions. Evie felt a rush of happiness. Once more the flashes had been accurate, and Evie began to trust them again. Everything was just as it should be.

A second date followed, then a third. They met each other's friends, then parents. After a couple of months they went on a testing camping holiday together in the Dales. They still liked each other after a week of rain and soggy groundsheets, smelly socks and snoring. A year later they were married, blissfully happy and planning their future together. They debated whether, and when, to have children. Evie felt loved, secure, almost indecently content with her life.

But less than three years later something happened that made her begin to suspect that there was a darker, dangerous side to her visions. Maybe the price of her happiness was paid for in the suffering of others.

Did she even have blood on her hands? Was she responsible for the deaths of two people, maybe more?

Her perfect life started to crumble.

CHAPTER THREE: ART

The first class started at ten the next morning, in one of the hotel's meeting rooms in the new wing. It was a bright room, with sunlight streaming in through the windows. The tables had been pushed together in the centre of the room, with the chairs in a circle around them. Yoghurt pots of water, kitchen rolls, pencils and rubbers had been set out. At the head of the table, a sheet of watercolour paper was taped to a board, and a camera was set up to project the page onto a screen on the wall behind. It was all reassuringly professional, thought Evie.

Their teacher, Aggie, greeted the amateur painters with a handshake as they entered. She was a small, round woman with a shock of curly, greying hair and a comfortable, easy manner.

'Come in, come in, take a seat everyone. I think we're all here. Great! Well, this morning we're going to go through some very basic principles of watercolour: wet and dry techniques, brush strokes, blending, et cetera, then this afternoon – the weather looks good – we'll go out in the field and do some mountain sketching. So, most of you met each other briefly for a drink yesterday, but maybe we could start today by going round the table, with each of you saying why you're here, what you like to paint, and where you're at with watercolour.' She gestured to George, the only man in the room.

'Hello, I'm George.' He was maybe in his mid sixties, tall, grey-haired, with a slightly defensive manner. 'I've been painting acrylics for years, but I've always wanted to have a go at watercolour. Every time I try on my own it's a disaster. This is my last ditch attempt, before I switch back to acrylics for good!'

'Well, there's a challenge!' smiled Aggie. She gestured to the next person, the elderly, unassuming lady in tweed skirt and cardigan.

'My name's Jean. I've been doing watercolours for quite a while – mainly flowers and birds, but I wanted to come to Scotland to try landscapes.' Evie had an idea that this woman would be very good, judging from the equipment set out before her: a palette which had seen years of use; each colour pan was half empty, and the mixing trays were a glorious muddle of bluey greys, earthy browns and greens.

The next person was a complete contrast. 'Hi, my name's Kayleigh and I've never painted before.' She was maybe in her mid-twenties, with long, poker-straight blonde hair, immaculate make-up and a Breton-style striped t-shirt that showed off her excellent figure. Her accent was southern English, maybe London or Essex. 'I watched all the Watercolour Challenge programmes on TV during lockdown, and thought I'd like to have a go. My dad got me all the gear for my birthday, so here I am!' Evie practically drooled with envy when she looked at the 'gear': the most expensive, the creamiest and richest Daniel Smith colours, and a set of immaculate sable brushes, still with their protective covers on. She guessed that Dad was either very rich, or very indulgent.

'I'm Fran. I've not painted before either, but I sketch and doodle a lot. I'm here to learn how to put colour onto my sketches. I'd like to start making travel sketchbooks one day.'

'My name's Helen,' said the next lady. She was a slight woman in her fifties, and wore jeans and a Shetland jumper. Her accent had an attractive touch of Geordie, but she looked a bit apprehensive and spoke with a tremor in her voice. 'I lost my husband last year, and really, I've been feeling a bit lost since then. I need to find a new activity. My children bought me this holiday as a Christmas gift. I'm probably going to be hopeless.'

'Not at all!' said Aggie, 'I promise you that by the end of the week you'll be doing some paintings your bairns will be really proud of.'

Then lastly it was Evie, who explained that she used to paint a lot, but hadn't for several years. 'This trip was Fran's idea,' she explained. 'She's my sister. She booked it up and presented me with a fait accompli. She says I need to get away and do something totally different for a few days, give myself a break. And it's nice to do something together; we don't get to see each other that often.' She smiled across the table at Fran.

'Well, a warm welcome to all of you. Now, we're going to start with a couple of exercises…'

The morning passed in a flash. Evie felt again how good it was to be totally engrossed in an activity, to the extent that no other thoughts could intrude. Last night's gruesome vision was completely forgotten. Aggie wandered round the table offering hints and gentle corrections, calming a frustrated George, and encouraging a timid Helen. It seemed that only minutes had passed before she said 'Right everyone, it's nearly one o'clock. We're going to have a break for lunch. Let's meet again in front of the hotel at 2pm. You just need your paints and brushes. Bring a warm jumper or a coat just in case. We'll supply the water, camping chairs, tea and coffee et cetera.'

'Where are we going?' asked George with a grumpy frown that seemed to be his trademark. 'Are we ready for open air, do you think?'

'Don't worry. I thought we'd start with something reasonably simple – the Black Cuillins. Nobody can really tell if your mountain is a bit wonky!'

'Did you enjoy that?' asked Fran as they filed out of the room and made their way to the dining room, where a buffet lunch had been put out.

'Brilliant!' enthused Evie. 'It's like art therapy. You're just totally in the zone, focused on a piece of paper as if it's the only thing that exists. What did you make of the others in the group?'

'I think George might be a bit of a pain. He kept throwing

his paintbrush down and swearing. Jean seems lovely, and Helen too.'

'What about Kayleigh? She looked like she'd be more at home on a Magaluf beach holiday to me. She's very pretty though.'

'Yeah, sure, if you like false eyelashes and lip fillers,' said Fran, a little meanly. 'I wonder how she'll get on sitting in the drizzly heather this afternoon!'

***

At two o'clock, the group were waiting in front of the hotel with Aggie when the minibus arrived with a crunch of gravel. Roddy jumped out and Evie muttered 'Oh, for God's sake' as she saw that he was wearing a faded kilt with his fisherman's sweater, long wool socks and hiking boots, 'It's bloody Brigadoon!' Fran snorted with laughter, which she disguised as a cough. Unaware of their mocking, Roddy smiled broadly and put out a hand to help the ladies into the vehicle.

They drove at a sedate pace along the single-track road, following the loch side towards the village of Carbost. Evie was glad not to be driving but Roddy seemed to read the road perfectly, knowing exactly when to pull in to a passing place, and when to let the oncoming cars pull over. Then they turned south towards Glenbrittle, and the dark, brooding mass of the Cuillins reappeared beyond the treeless hillsides. The road became still narrower, bordered by a fence on one side and a ditch on the other. The traffic here was heavier, with four or five vehicles attempting to pull in to each passing place. Often Roddy had to squeeze the van onto the soft verges or drive dangerously close to the ditch. Then they entered an area of pine forest, and the black mountains temporarily disappeared from view. Roddy swore as he found the next passing place blocked by two enormous camper vans and was forced to reverse back. Once through the forest, Evie gasped in surprise. The mountains were suddenly straight in front of them, massive and imposing, and they had changed colour. The foothills were a dark mossy green, and the peaks were now blueish purple. She began to itch to get her paints out and capture that exact colour, but the drive had become slower and slower, as they found themselves in a long queue of cars and camper vans.

'We're really near the Fairy Pools,' Roddy explained in his soft, lilting brogue, which, to Evie, sounded similar to an Irish accent. Despite her initial negative impression of this man, she found the way he rolled his Rs quite appealing. 'Everyone wants to go there for some reason. It'll be ok once we're past the turn-off.'

Evie noticed that the narrow road was now bordered on one side by red and white poles, spaced barely a couple of metres apart. 'Are those snow poles?' she asked. 'Do you get much snow here?'

'No, they're to stop idiots parking on the side of the road. It used to be practically impossible to get by on this road before they did that.'

'So where do people park?'

'They built a new car park. It's a monstrosity, a real scar on the landscape. And even that gets full by mid-morning. People get into fights trying to snatch the last places. And all to see some waterfalls that you could see in a hundred other places on Skye. It's pure madness.'

As they approached the turn-off to the car park, Evie could see that cars and vans were queueing to get in. Roddy managed to weave the minivan past the queue, and at last they were past the turn-off and free of traffic. A little further on, they pulled into a small parking space and Roddy stopped the engine.

'OK, we're here', said Aggie. 'Sorry that took so long. If we walk just a few metres up this footpath, you'll see the most amazing view. Could you all grab a camping chair? Roddy can take the drinks.'

The view was stunning. A wall of rock rose up before them, with five distinct jagged peaks, separated by a maze of deep crevasses and treacherous tumbles of scree. The rocks shone purple, grey, blue and black in the afternoon sunshine. The olive-coloured foothills swept away towards brighter green pastures, interrupted by boulders and the occasional sheep. The group stood in awe for a few minutes, then began to scout about for the perfect viewpoint to set up their chairs and materials.

After an hour, Evie felt she'd finished. She knew if she carried on fiddling she'd ruin the painting. She glanced over at the others, still heads down, concentrating – all except Kayleigh, who'd wandered off in her fashionable white boots to smoke a cigarette. Evie closed her paintbox, washed her brushes and walked over to where Roddy was sitting on a rock, carving a piece of wood with his sgian dubh, the traditional small Scottish dagger. He looked ridiculously macho, thought Evie, with his wavy reddish hair, his hairy knees splayed apart and his hands busy whittling away at the piece of wood in his lap. He could be an extra in Braveheart, she thought, sourly. He just needed a bit of blue war paint. He looked up as she approached and gave her a friendly smile.

'You finished already then?'

'Yeah, the most difficult thing is knowing when to stop. I've ruined a lot of paintings by just tweaking and tweaking.'

'Can I get you a drink? We've got tea, black coffee, cokes and water.'

'Oh, tea would be lovely, thanks.'

'It's with milk, is that OK?'

'Perfect.' Evie sat on another rock and held the hot tea in both hands to warm her fingers. The weather was changing, and a chill wind had started to blow. The mountains were gradually losing their purplish sheen, and were once more returning to daunting shades of slate grey and black.

'So, what do you think of the Black Cuillins then?' asked Roddy.

'Honestly? I think they're terrifying. The scale of them. The sharpness of the peaks. I can't imagine anyone attempting to climb them.'

'You'd do right to be frightened. It's a dangerous climb. The ridges are narrow as fuck and the rocks are frost-shattered and unstable. And your compass won't work because the rock is magnetic. And then there's the weather...'

'Jesus, why would anyone even try?'

'Ah, but the views are something else! Like nothing else in the world.'

'Are you a climber, then?'

'Aye, my real job's mountain guide, and I'm sometimes a fishing guide too.'

'So how did you end up with this soft gig, shepherding a bunch of watercolour ladies – and one man - around the island?'

'Aggie's a good pal of my auntie, so I couldna really refuse. But it's no so bad. I get to stay at the hotel for free so it's a wee holiday for me.'

'So you work with tourists all the time. What do you make of the protests? We got stopped at the bridge for ages yesterday.'

His face darkened and Evie caught a brief flash of anger, before his normal smile returned. 'Well, there's different types of tourist,' he said. 'People like you, and the climbers, and the fishermen, they take time to look at the scenery and treat it with respect. But the selfie-takers, the cruise ship passengers, them I could do without.'

Evie found herself reluctantly warming to this man, with his obvious pride in his surroundings. Maybe he wasn't such a fake after all, she thought. She was about to ask him if he was born here, when Aggie called out: 'I think we'd better start packing up now, everyone. The sky's looking a bit ominous.'

***

Back at the hotel, after a quick wash and change, Evie and Fran went down to the bar for a pre-dinner drink.

'I saw you chatting up the hunk earlier on. Have you changed your mind about him?' asked Fran.

'Yeah, I have a bit. I think maybe he's the genuine article, a soft-spoken Highland gentleman. He seems very passionate about Skye.'

'You should have seen the way Kayleigh was scowling at you both – I think she's got the hots for him.'

'She's welcome to him; he's nice enough but he's not my type at all. What was her painting like, by the way, did you get a look at it? I only saw Jean's and that was amazing.'

'Um, how can I put it without being cruel… Naif? Graphic? You'll see it tomorrow when we do a feedback session. You grab those seats over there and I'll get the drinks. Wine?'

'Can you get me a Baileys with ice?'

There were a handful of people in the bar; a group of four hill walkers with muddy boots, the American couple - Evie gave a small wave – and a tall, slim man dressed in black who was hunched over his laptop. Evie sat down in the deep velvet armchair with a contented sigh. She noticed a newspaper on the table in front of her, the Press and Journal, and pulled it towards her. The front page showed a photo of the anti-tourism protestors at the Skye bridge, and Evie devoured the article with interest.

'Hey, thanks!' she said, when Fran returned with the drinks. 'This article is fascinating. It's talking about the protests. I had no idea they were getting so violent. Listen to this: '*Anti-tourism rhetoric has been ramping up of late, and some protesters have been involved in direct action. Airbnb guests throughout the island woke up this morning to find their doors had been painted* with 'Go Home'. Several camper vans at the Stighan campsite found their tyres had been slashed in the night. Protesters last week lined the Portree dock and jeered as the three thousand passengers disembarked from the Dutch cruise ship Sea Legend. Local resident Harry Mackay said 'I've got every sympathy for the protesters; our island is becoming one giant theme park. We want visitors, but quality visitors. Ones who stay a decent time. Not the day-trippers who jump out their car, take a selfie in front of the old Sligachan bridge and don't even turn round to look at it before racing off to the next spot. Not these cruise ships spewing out thousands that jump into buses, clog up the roads then go back to the ships for their dinner. And the camper vans – worst of all. Ruining our roads, throwing out litter and going to the toilet wherever they damn please – if you ask me, that bridge should never have been built!'

'Wow, it makes you feel a bit uncomfortable, doesn't it? I wonder if we qualify as 'quality visitors'?' said Fran.

'I guess we do, cos we're staying for more than a week.'

'I wonder if there's anything in the paper about the murder?' Fran said.

Evie carefully turned the pages, scanning each headline. 'Yes,' she said, eventually, 'on page six, I'll read it out: *Highlands and Islands Police say they are following an important lead in the murder of French influencer Florence Escoffier, aged 29. Chief Inspector Michael McLennan stated: 'We are confident that an arrest will soon be made. The general public should be assured that events such as this are incredibly rare on the island, which is considered to be amongst the safest places in Great Britain.'*

Evie became aware that the tall, thin man was no longer engrossed in his laptop, but was staring at them fixedly from the next table. His eyes were an intense and unsettling black, like deep pools of nothingness, completely devoid of expression. 'Do you mind if I see that,' he asked in a crisp, cultured English accent.

'Um, yeah, go ahead.'

She held out the paper and the man practically snatched it from her fingers before returning to his seat and devouring the short article, a frown on his face.

Fran was intrigued. She dared to lean over and ask: 'Are you interested in the murder?'

The man looked up, surprised, and seemed to take a moment to compose himself before replying: 'Yes, I am. I'm a writer. I'm researching a book about myths and ancient beliefs on Skye. This murder struck me as ritualistic, the way the body was displayed with the arms crossed. It reminded me of the pagan rites of the Druids.' Having previously been staring at them, he now seemed unable to meet their eyes. His manner became brusque and tense, as if he regretted talking so much.

The sisters introduced themselves.

'Arthur Ross,' he replied, curtly.

'So would we have read any of your books?' Evie asked.

'I doubt it,' he replied, a little patronisingly. 'They're quite academic. The last one was about the Highland Clearances on Skye.' Evie was put out that he assumed they would not read academic literature, but feigned interest with a lift of her eyebrows.

'Really? That sounds fascinating.'

'I did some of the research for it here in the hotel. The Minister of the Manse played a big part in the evictions from the villages on the shore. The local Laird made him encourage the villagers to leave, and then their houses were burnt down, so there was no going back. Hundreds died on the ships going over to the colonies.' He looked annoyed, as if he felt Evie had trapped him into a discussion. 'Well, excuse me, ladies, I must go.' With that, he slammed his laptop shut, rose from his seat and stalked off.

Evie noticed that he'd left his whisky half finished. 'Strange man!' she murmured.

'I think he's maybe on the spectrum,' replied Fran. 'That

intensity, the lack of social skills, the way he couldn't look at us when he was speaking. We'll have to google him! See if he's famous.'

'I think he's just rude,' said Evie. 'But it's strange what he just said. I had a vision about the murder last night,' she admitted. 'It was pretty grim. I got the feeling it was ritualistic too.'

'Did you?' Fran never questioned the visions. 'Why's that?'

'The body was definitely posed. The hair was brushed out straight behind the head and the hands were crossed over the chest. It reminded me a bit of those medieval brass rubbings.'

Fran nodded thoughtfully. 'Well, try not to focus on it too much. It sounds like the police are going to catch the guy soon. We've had a great day today, and we've got nine more to come. It's all good! Cheers!'

The sisters clinked glasses and relaxed back into their seats.

CHAPTER FOUR: THE HOUSE

Jake had always been uncomfortable when Evie talked about the flashes. It was as if he felt excluded by them, aware that it was something they could not fully share. When she'd told him she'd known at Becca's wedding that he was the one, he'd reacted strangely.

'What's up?' she'd asked. 'You look at bit put out.'

'Well, it's like I don't have any agency in it. I mean, it was me who phoned you, it was my idea to meet again. You make it sound like I was drawn into your web like some daft little spider!'

Jake was a down-to-earth man. He had no truck with alternative medicine, any kind of therapy, or even osteopathy. He was straightforward, totally honest and kind. Evie adored him, but had learned over the years to keep her visions to herself.

After two happy years in rented accommodation, their joint belongings squeezed into a two-bed flat, they decided to start house-hunting. They decided to focus on the Wakefield area, between her job in Leeds, and his job as a mechanic in Huddersfield. They'd visited dozens of neat little semis in Sandal, or Ossett or Horbury, before finding the ideal property one day near Newmillerdam, a village on the outskirts of Wakefield with a fine country park on the doorstep. It was a terraced cottage built of Yorkshire stone and covered in ivy. There was a small front garden, and a bigger back garden that sloped down to woodland. It was a financial stretch, but with a little help from their parents they could just about afford it. And Evie knew. As soon as she pushed open the gate, she knew that they would live here. She saw that they would repaint the living room a light mushroom brown. She knew that they would replace the swing in the garden with a vegetable planter. She was confident and carefree as they phoned the estate agent with their offer.

Jake was heartbroken the next day when they found out that the house had been sold to another young couple. They had been outbid. But Evie was not worried. They would get the house; and sure enough, a couple of weeks later the estate agency rang to tell them that the other couple had pulled out, and did they still want to go ahead with their offer?

The next six months were the happiest in Evie's life. They spent their weekends pulling up weeds and repainting the walls. They discovered pretty local walks and had bar lunches in the village pubs. Fran came to stay from London, and was entranced by the little cottage and its leafy surroundings. And then one day it all came crashing down.

Evie and Jake were invited to a barbeque one summer evening at Alice and Mike's house next-door. They had spoken to their elderly neighbours several times over the garden fence, or in the street, but this was the first occasion where they'd spent any time with them. As Jake helped Mike with the barbeque, Evie and Alice sat on the patio with drinks and chatted. Then Alice dropped the bombshell.

'I'm so glad to have you and Jake as neighbours. It's lovely to have young people on the street. Of course, it was a dreadful shame about that other couple.'

'What couple is that,' asked Evie, distractedly, as she watched Jake turning the sausages. He was concentrating hard on not dropping them. I love that man, she thought. He looks so serious, he cares so much.

'The ones who were going to buy the house before you.'

'Why, what happened to them?' asked Evie, beginning to feel uneasy.

'Didn't you hear? They were both killed in a car crash. It

was the same day they had their offer accepted. It was just dreadful.'

Evie felt as if her chest was being hollowed out. She struggled to breathe.

'I had no idea,' she gasped. 'That's awful.' Somehow she managed to get through the evening. She ate, she chatted and she thanked Alice and Mike for a lovely night. But once home she collapsed onto the sofa and sobbed. Jake hovered over her, helpless, patting her shoulder, saying over and over 'What is it, Evie? What's wrong?'

'It's… it's the couple who were going to buy this house before us,' said Evie, when she was at last able to talk. 'They died in a car crash.'

'Shit. That's awful.'

'The same day they made the offer on the house.'

'Terrible. But it's nothing to do with us, surely.'

'But don't you see? I knew. I knew we'd get this house.'

'OK, you had one of your feelings. That's normal, everyone envisages themselves in a house they really like. It doesn't mean anything.'

'But it's happened before. I think I make things happen.'

'Don't be daft, Evie, that's impossible. How is it physically possible? You don't even know who they were!'

'Things just happen so I get what I want. It's not the first time.'

'It's pure coincidence, Evie.'

'No, listen. A party I really don't want to go to – it gets cancelled. A gig I really want to go to that's sold out – someone rings with tickets they can't use. Oh, lots of things. The promotion at work - Becca should have got it, but she pulled out.'

'Yes, because she wanted to concentrate on the new baby. This stuff just happens, Evie, it's not you who makes it happen.'

'Let me ask you this, then. I've never asked you this before.

When we met at Becca's wedding, you had a girlfriend. What happened to her?'

'I told you, she went back to Cardiff. She's Welsh.'

'But why did she go back?'

'Evie, stop it, it's…'

'Why?' she insisted, raising her voice.

Jake was silent for a moment. Then he admitted: 'Her mum got cancer. She wanted to be near her.'

'There! There, you see?'

'No! I don't see anything.' Jake sat down heavily on the sofa and put his head in his hands. He sighed.

'Look,' he said, 'Let's be logical. It's not possible to change events. What happens, happens, it's totally random. But maybe it's possible to have a premonition. Even I could maybe believe that you had like a flash of déjà vu when you came into this house.'

'It's not déjà vu, it's future vu – I saw what colour we'd paint the walls, I knew what we'd plant in the garden.'

'Yeah, that's normal, so did I. That's called imagination.'

They argued on through the night, with Evie convinced that some dark malevolent force had gifted them the house, but Jake refusing to entertain the idea, desperate to persuade her that it was just an unhappy coincidence. Finally, exhausted, they went to bed.

Over the next weeks and months, Evie found her feelings about the house starting to change. She didn't deserve it. She'd got it through deceitful means and could no longer enjoy it. All the things she had loved about it now gave her no joy. She became withdrawn, cautious, not daring to hope or plan in case her dreams impacted others. She was reluctant to make any decisions, relying on Jake to decide where they would holiday, or what car they might buy. Every action on her part seemed to have a possible negative consequence, and so she avoided as much as she could. 'Whatever, I don't mind, you choose!' became her standard reply to any tricky question, to Jake's growing exasperation. She became a pale imitation of her former self, her confidence and vitality slowly draining away.

Jake was at first sympathetic, but over time he became frustrated and resentful. It seemed to him that all the personality had washed out of the woman he loved, leaving him with someone he hardly recognised. Their once perfect relationship started to show strain. They snapped at each other more and more. Evie knew she had to do something. If they were to survive this, she had to find out if she had some kind of psychic power or not.

But the action she finally took didn't save their marriage; it turned out to be the last nail in the coffin for Jake.

CHAPTER FIVE: RAIN

It poured down the next morning. When Evie opened her curtains she saw that the Black Cuillins had disappeared behind a wall of cloud and the rain was lashing down almost horizontally, spattering noisily against the window. She knocked on Fran's door and they went down to breakfast together.

'You look a bit bleary-eyed this morning,' said Fran.

'Yeah, I didn't sleep too well. Funny dreams,' admitted Evie.

'Well let's see if a double espresso will sort you out.'

Ten o'clock saw them back in the art room. The group were to spend the morning working on perspectives in architecture and the multiple colours that can coexist in stone walls, ready for a what would have been an afternoon of outdoor painting. The subject was supposed to be a deserted old schoolhouse in the hills. But Aggy warned them that the trip would have to be cancelled.

'The forecast is not that great, I'm afraid,' she said. 'It's getting better, and there'll be some periods of sunshine but they'll be interspersed with pretty heavy showers. Plus there's quite a strong wind today. I think we'd have real difficulty outdoors. Never fear, this often happens and we have a contingency plan. Here's what we'll do instead. I have a whole stack of architectural photos – crofts, castles, ruins, cottages. You can choose your favourite and we'll work in here this afternoon. But before we start on perspectives, let's look at what each of us produced yesterday. Constructive criticism only please!'

Nervously, the group laid their paintings out on the table, and one by one Aggy gave them advice.

'It's not good enough,' George had grumbled. 'Look at the sky, it's all patchy!'

'You can sort that out; just wet that part of the paper again and put another wash over it.'

'No, it's ruined,' said George, angrily, turning the painting over to hide it.

Helen was quietly pleased with what she'd produced, and everyone lavished praises on her gentle, delicate watercolour. 'Brilliant start,' enthused Aggie. 'The next step is to try and be a little bolder with your colours. Don't forget that watercolour paint always dries a couple of shades lighter.'

Fran was next. 'Very nice work, very detailed, nice cross-hatching with your pencil. I think your style might be more suited to line and wash. You might try experimenting with doing your sketch in ink rather than pencil next time.'

'Evie, a good strong start, nice bold colours. Why did you add the little farmhouse?'

'I wanted to give an idea of scale. Otherwise you'd have no idea how massive the mountains are.'

'I see! Yes, everyone, don't be too literal. Feel free to add things, or take things away, to make your composition work. Kayleigh, wow, you're prolific!'

Kayleigh had gone through four sheets of the most expensive Arches watercolour paper with pure, vivid splashes of unblended colours, and Evie actually quite liked them; they were bold and abstract, even if it was hard to tell what they were meant to be. But Kayleigh was unimpressed. 'I dunno,' she said, 'this painting lark's not as easy as I thought it would be. And there's a lot of just sitting and staring. God, my arse got so sore yesterday. Do we have to come to all the sessions? I'd like to go into Portree and look at the shops one day.'

Aggie looked taken aback, but recovered quickly. 'Of

course. This is your holiday, and you can do whatever you like. But don't give up on painting. It takes a little time before you see results.'

Jean's painting was magnificent. Evie would have happily had it on her wall. Secretly, she thought Jean a slightly better artist than their teacher, and wondered if Aggie was a little defensive when she commented: 'Maybe a touch too heavy on the shadow in the crevasses. If I were you I'd get a clean, damp brush and lift some of the colour out of these bits. Right then,' she continued, 'It's wonderful to see so many different styles and interpretations. Thank you all for sharing. Now, let's have a little talk about perspectives, the rule of thirds and vanishing points.'

The morning passed quickly again and Evie enjoyed all the little exercises. Before she knew it, it was time for lunch.

When they entered the dining room, Evie and Fran were beckoned over to a table where Marge and Brett were sitting, their plates piled high with food.

'Hello you two! How's the painting going?' asked Marge.

'Oh, pretty good! We're learning lots. How's the whisky tasting?'

'Very enjoyable. We took a ferry to the isle of Raasay yesterday and looked at the new distillery there. They're making some delicious young whiskies – and there are wonderful views too,' said Brett.

'And what's on your programme for this afternoon?' asked Evie.

'We thought we'd do some history for a change. My ancestors came over from Scotland in the clearances. Not from Skye, they came from the Isle of Lewis, but we thought we'd visit some of the old clearance villages, and then maybe see some ruined castles and brochs. Margie needs a break from whisky!'

'Oh, you should talk to that guy, um, what was his name? Arthur something. Yes, Arthur Ross, I think. He's written a book about the Skye clearances.'

'Has he?' asked Brett, 'Well, we must pick his brains before we set off.'

Marge pursed her lips. 'Oh, that man,' she said. 'He's a strange fish. There's something not quite right about him.'

'What makes you say that?' asked Fran.

'He's an eavesdropper, for one thing. When that poor girl got murdered and the police came round to interview us, we all went into a meeting room, you see, one by one, and we saw him hanging around outside with his ear to the door. He scuttled off when he saw us. But there's something creepy about him.'

'So he was staying here when it happened?'

'Yes he was. I wouldn't be surprised if...'

'Marge!' admonished her husband. 'You mustn't gossip!'

'Who else was at the hotel at the time, who's still here now?' asked Evie. Fran shot her a questioning look.

'That group of fell walkers. And the handsome boy, Robbie.'

'You mean Roddy?'

'Yes, that's right.'

'But why did the police interview people here in the hotel? Was there a connection to the girl?'

'Not that I know of,' said Brett. 'I know they talked to the manager and he confirmed she wasn't a guest here. But the churchyard where she was found is probably only a mile's walk away. I guess they thought we might have seen her – I know they talked a lot with the hill walkers who'd been out all day.'

After lunch, when Evie and Fran were heading back to the art room in the modern wing of the hotel, Fran asked:

'Why did you ask Marge and Brett who was in the hotel that's still here today?'

'I dunno really. I'm still thinking about that vision I got of the victim and wondering if it means I'm supposed to know something, or do something.'

'Have you had the vision again?'

'No. But last night I had this weird feeling of being trapped somewhere cold and damp. Like an old railway tunnel or something. Curved stone walls.'

'I don't think there's any railways on Skye, are there?'

'Oh, no, you're right, probably not. So it must be nothing. Just a dream.'

'Probably all the Baileys you drank last night! You were really going for it!'

'Yes, I was a bit. '

'Drowning your sorrows?' asked Fran, gently.

'No, not at all. It's great being here, Fran, I'm loving the art lessons, I'm loving the views, and I'm loving being here with you!' She gave her sister a quick hug before they pushed open the door.

And Evie loved the afternoon too. She chose a photo of a deliciously decayed old croft, with green mould growing up the blackened walls, gaping holes where windows had once been, and a rusted red tin roof, partly collapsed. It stood on the hillside overlooking the rugged coastline, and the sky behind it was pregnant with dark clouds. Blues and greys and muddy greens – all of Evie's favourite colours. There's beauty in decay, she thought. She wondered who had lived in the croft and why they had abandoned it. Once again, she finished quickly. She looked around, seeing Fran still intent on her detailed drawing, George huffing to himself, Aggie sitting beside Helen, correcting a pencil line. Suddenly Evie felt very tired.

'Aggie, I think I've finished,' she said. 'Is it ok if I slope off early?'

'Yes, of course it is! Go and put your feet up.'

'I think I'll go too,' said Kayleigh, rising from her seat. 'I'm just making mine worse.'

Evie held the door open for Kayleigh, and the two women

left the room and walked down the corridor towards the main hotel.

'God, I need some fresh air,' said Kayleigh. 'And I'm dying for a fag. All we do is sit on those bloody hard chairs. My legs have gone all jumpy.'

Evie suddenly felt sorry for this young woman, so far out of her comfort zone, forced to spend time with people she had nothing in common with.

'Fancy some company?' she asked. 'We could walk round the gardens?'

Kayleigh looked surprised, but pleased. 'Yeah, sure,' she said.

They pushed the heavy fire door open and walked towards the stable block and the formal walled gardens that lay behind. Kayleigh got out her cigarettes.

'Fancy one?' she asked.

'No, I don't... oh, why they hell not!' said Evie. 'I haven't smoked for years but I remember how much I used to like it.'

They walked and smoked in comfortable silence for a few minutes. Then Evie asked:

'So are you enjoying this painting holiday?'

'Honestly? No, not really. It's not my thing at all.'

'Why did you sign up for it?'

'Oh, it was my dad. He keeps buying me stuff. I had a horsey phase when I was a kid, like most girls do, and he bought me a fucking horse. Way too big and too powerful for me, scared the shit out of me.'

'Well, nice to have a generous dad, I suppose.'

'Nah, it's guilt. He's on the telly, doesn't have enough time to spend on me, so he spends his money instead,' said Kayleigh, bluntly.

'He's on the TV? What does he do?'

'He's Hugo Petersen.'

'You mean the TV chef? Wow, he's famous!'

'Yeah,' Kayleigh gave a short, bitter laugh. 'Rich and famous. We have a lovely house, fabulous holidays. I could have anything I wanted, within reason, and I have absolutely no fucking idea what to do with my life.'

'But you're so young. How old are you, if you don't mind me asking?'

'Twenty-six. And you?'

'I'm pushing thirty. Not so different from you, really. But separated from my husband, depressed, no kids, living in a pokey flat... You've got everything still in front of you. You'll be fine.'

Kayleigh smiled. 'Thanks. I hope so. Sorry about your husband.'

Evie shrugged and turned towards the mountains to hide the tears that always threatened when Jake was mentioned. 'That's why I'm here really,' she said. 'It might seem boring here to you, but for me it's a relief after a really shit year. I can just switch off here.'

'Well, there's one thing that's not boring,' said Kayleigh with a sideways glance. 'I wonder what Roddy's doing with his day off?'

'You like him, don't you?'

'He's OK. I mean, I've got to liven up this bloody holiday somehow, don't I?' She flicked her long poker-straight blonde hair behind her ears and shot Evie another side-long glance, then gave a wide grin. It was the first time Evie had seen her without her normal apathetic, slightly sulky expression, and her whole face lit up. She really is quite beautiful, she thought.

Evi laughed. 'You do! You go for it, girl!' she said, happy that she'd made Kayleigh smile.

'I think I'm going back in now. I'm going to check out the

41

bar, see if he's in there. Thanks for… um, well, just thanks.'

'Good luck,' said Evie, and surprised herself by giving Kayleigh a light hug.

Evie sat on a bench and smiled to herself. She's a nice girl, she thought. Behind those model good looks and designer clothes, she's just as mixed up as the rest of us. But there's barely four years between us, and I feel a million times older than her; old and worn-out and jaded. If only I hadn't lied to Jake. If only I'd been up-front about where I was going.

But regrets were useless. It was all much too late.

C HAPTER SIX: GLASGOW

After just a couple of hours of Googling one morning, when Jake was out helping a friend change his car battery, Evie thought she'd found what she was looking for. She'd put 'parapsychology research UK' in the search engine, and had trawled through several hits. Some centres were obviously dubious; the ones which offered evenings with mediums or expensive private readings, but there were three bona fide university research groups, in York, London and Glasgow. She examined each one carefully, looking at the qualifications of the staff, the quality of the research publications they had produced, and the number of current research projects. One stood out: Glasgow University Parapsychology Unit. The staff were mainly psychologists with many years of experience, and there were several PhD projects ongoing. The unit seemed to focus on clinical trials and when Evie read the sentence 'testing whether people have psychic abilities in a controlled laboratory environment', she knew she'd hit the jackpot. She also liked the fact that the Unit offered counselling on how to cope with paranormal phenomena.

She phoned immediately, but was asked to write a detailed email to a certain Dr Sarah Caulfield, who specialised in ESP - specifically mind-reading and precognition. Once she'd pressed 'send' on the email, Evie felt a huge surge of relief. She had taken action. She could hopefully get some help and begin to understand what was happening to her. She tossed up whether or not to tell Jake, but decided to wait and see if anything came of her email enquiry first.

Evie was stunned to get a reply only a couple of weeks later, asking if she was available to come up to Glasgow in the next month or so to take part in a week of tests. Evie knew she should talk to Jake about this, but could imagine only too well what he would say. 'Bunch of charlatans' and 'You shouldn't mess around with this, it could make things worse.' He might even succeed in making her change her mind. Evie herself had googled 'dangers of exploring psychic abilities' and had been upset to read the words 'depression, obsession, delusion, detachment from reality.' But on the other hand, she felt she absolutely had to know whether what she had been experiencing were just premonitions, or whether she had the power to influence outcomes.

Evie formed a plan. She had an old university friend, Polly, who was living in Helensburgh, just north of Glasgow. Jake would remember her from the wedding, when she'd got spectacularly drunk and had knocked over a tower of champagne glasses. She could make up a half-true story for Jake – that her friend was maybe going through some kind of trauma and needed her help. Jake was so trusting, so honest. He wouldn't question her if she said she needed to go there. Jake would probably put her on the train, but instead of changing stations for Helensburgh, she'd get off in Glasgow, find a cheap Airbnb there and spend as much time as she could at the Unit.

It all worked out exactly as she'd hoped. Jake had driven her to the station, carried her luggage onto the platform, kissed her and waved as the train pulled out. Evie felt awash with guilt as she watched his figure receding into the distance, but then a spark of optimism as she reread the correspondence from Dr Caulfield.

The tests were intriguing, and Evie threw herself into them with an open mind. In some she was asked to sit in a darkened room with a mask and noise-cancelling headphones on, and mentally project a series of random images that she had chosen herself to a receiving student in another room. Then the process was reversed, so that Evie strained to see images being sent to her telepathically. In another exercise, Evie and Dr Caulfield sat opposite each other. In front of the doctor, but facing Evie, were twelve cards with simple images: a star, a dog, a fish, etc. Evie was asked to guess which image would be selected by the doctor and to write the word on a sheet numbered one to twelve, before the doctor chose an image. This process was also reversed, with Evie choosing the images and the doctor guessing in advance. There followed tests on clairvoyance, with objects being hidden under a not very scientific looking flower pot, and telekinesis, with Evie attempting to make water in a glass tremble, or make a ball roll across a table.

Towards the end of the week, Evie discussed the results with Dr Caulfield.

'Well,' started the doctor, 'this has been a really interesting week. You came here very disturbed by visions. You were unsure whether these were precognition – that is, premonitions - or whether you had some form of telekinesis – the ability to move objects or change events through mental powers. We also tested your powers of telepathy and clairvoyance. Most of the tests produced a very standard result - a thirty percent or under success rate, which can be classed as non-paranormal. You do not have any particular telepathic ability. However, one test was interesting.

'The test in which you had to predict which object I chose, and write the word down, showed a success rate of eighty percent, which is much higher than average and, to me, shows psychic ability. The question remains, however, did you predict the card chosen, or did you influence my choice in some way.

'Now, let's assume that you have precognition. Let's try and isolate this a bit further. Can you answer these questions: First, do the visions come suddenly, out of the blue, or when you're thinking about something specific?'

'Very suddenly. Completely out of the blue.'

'And what degree of certainty do you feel about the premonition, on a scale of one to ten?'

'Ten. Every time.'

'Do the visions make you feel confused?'

'No, not usually.'

'Do you experience any physical markers when you have a vision - like a feeling of chill, or restlessness?'

'No, not really.'

'OK, thank you.' Dr Caulfield looked at her notes, wrote down a few observations, and then looked up at Evie with a smile.

'So what's the verdict, doctor?'

'The evidence would suggest that you have one form of ESP, and that is precognition, the ability to occasionally foresee events. The fact that you show absolutely no telekinetic ability would to me imply no ability to make things happen through conscious or unconscious thought control.'

'But you can't discount it?'

'Let me just say, that in over twenty years of parapsychological research, I have never come across an individual with that kind of psychic ability.'

'So the things I was worrying about, the woman I hated who broke her leg the next day...'

'Most probably coincidence.'

'Recognising the man I was going to marry?'

'Premonition. A nice one.'

'And the fact that his girlfriend's mum got cancer?'

'I would put that down to sheer bad luck.'

'OK, and the certainty about my house? And the couple who were killed?'

'Premonition or even just wishful thinking. And as for the couple, I would say it is just a very unfortunate coincidence. I've pencilled you in for a couple of sessions with our clinical psychologist tomorrow. That should help put these thoughts into perspective and hopefully ease your mind on that score.'

Evie left Glasgow feeling like a new person, lighter, more positive, ready to throw her arms round Jake and do everything possible to get their relationship back to where it was. She'd phoned and texted him during her stay in Glasgow, each time making vague statements about how her friend Polly was improving, and inventing outings to fish and chip restaurants and museums.

Jake was not at the station to meet her. He wasn't answering his mobile either. Evie got a taxi home, feeling a growing sense of trepidation. She found Jake sitting in the kitchen, in the dark, nursing a glass of beer. He looked up at her with eyes that were frighteningly cold.

'Where've you been?' he asked in a controlled voice.

'Helensburgh. I...'

'Don't lie to me!' he thundered. 'I phoned Polly. She was in your address book. You've been lying to me all week! Are you having an affair?'

'No! Oh no, of course not!'

'Then where were you?'

'I... I went to Glasgow University. I did a week of tests on ESP. I knew you wouldn't approve, so I didn't tell you. I'm so sorry.'

'For Christ's sake, Evie!'

'But listen, it was good! I know a lot more now. The tests were reassuring and...'

'But you lied to me!' he shouted once again. 'I don't care about the fucking tests. You lied to me!'

'I'm sorry, I should have...'

'You can sleep in the spare room tonight,' said Jake, and with that he rose from his chair, swallowed the last of his beer and stalked out of the room.

Over the next few days Evie tried desperately to talk to Jake, to make him understand why she'd gone and how important the tests had been for her. But each time, Jake made excuses to leave the room and refused to engage with her. Then one day, he did open up.

'Sit down, Evie, we need to talk.'

At last, thought Evie. We can get somewhere now. She smiled nervously and began the speech she'd been mentally preparing:

'I am so sorry I didn't tell you before I went. It was….'

But Jake cut her off with a gesture.

'Evie, I love you. But I feel like I don't know you any more. You've changed so much. It's like I woke up one morning and there was a different person in my bed. You've been apathetic and miserable, for months. You don't want to do anything, you don't seem to enjoy our life together. I thought it was depression, I wanted to give you time and space to get better. But this last thing, this Glasgow thing… I don't know. I didn't think you were capable of lying like that.'

'I'm sorry Jake.'

Then he said, baldly: 'I can't be with you like this.'

'What? No, Jake, please…'

'I'm sorry. I think we should have a break. I want you to stay with your parents for a while, then we'll see where we're at.'

'You want me to move out?' said Evie, stupidly.

'Yes. For a while. Then we'll see.'

'But that's so drastic. We surely don't need to…'

'It's what I want.'

And so Evie had packed a suitcase and phoned her parents. She felt embarrassed and ashamed to be living with her parents again, sleeping in her childhood bedroom, watching game shows with her mum and dad in the evening. They were shocked, but supportive. They treated her with extreme kindness and a tentative protectiveness that Evie found almost unbearable; she would have preferred them to question, to blame, to argue. But they moved around her with a kind of frightened cautiousness, as if Evie might shatter if confronted. The days passed slowly, but turned into weeks, then a month passed. Evie went to work at the council every day as normal, holding things together and putting on a brave face, but at night she cried. She phoned Jake a couple of times, and went to fetch some belongings from the house, but he was still distant with her.

Then one day she pushed open the door to her open-plan office and found Becca, back from maternity leave, putting a photo of her baby daughter on her desk and chatting to the others about the difficulties in finding a childminder. Evie felt awkward; this was Jake's cousin, and she was bound to have an opinion about the break-up. They smiled at each other, but Evie sensed a certain coldness. At lunchtime they found themselves in the same queue at the sandwich shop.

'It's nice to have you back,' said Evie, brightly. 'Was it hard to leave the baby?'

'Yes, really hard. But it's a mixture of guilt and relief to be back in the real world again. How are you?'

'Oh, you know... OK.' Then she said, with a burst of honesty: 'Actually I'm doing crap. I love Jake. I'd do anything to get back together. Have you heard from him?'

Becca gave her a pitying look. 'Yes. He came round for dinner last week.' She paused, then added: 'I'm sorry Evie; he brought his new girlfriend with him.'

Evie gasped, stunned. Her heart started beating too fast and her throat felt constricted. She was having trouble breathing. She turned and ran out of the shop, gasping for air. Once around the corner, she leant her hips against a brick wall and rested with her head down, her hand on her chest.

'Are you alright, luv?' asked a passer-by.

Evie managed a nod and the woman continued down the street.

That evening she started to look for a flat to rent.

CHAPTER SEVEN: MISSING

'How are you this morning?' asked Fran as they walked down the stairs to breakfast. 'It was a fantastic night last night wasn't it? Are you feeling as hung-over as I am?'

'No, I'm not too bad actually. I drank water most of the night; I was so thirsty! You?'

'Pretty grim. My head's still thumping.'

The hotel had organised a little ceilidh the previous evening in the dining room. Tables had been pushed to the walls and chairs arranged in a circle to create a decent sized dance area. A local band had arrived with a fiddler, an accordionist and a drummer, and one of the hotel waitresses acted as 'caller', walking the guests through the steps and shouting out instructions once the music started. The tunes were fast and energetic, the dancing wild and the laughter raucous, as the guests stumbled though the steps. The four hill walkers turned out to be good company, pulling the at-first reluctant ladies onto the dance floor. Roddy was also on fine form, his kilt swirling as he span to the Gay Gordons and the Dashing White Seargeant. Evie had a wonderful night. Kayleigh was much in demand too. 'This is my dance! Kayleigh's at the ceilidh!' she yelled at Evie as they span away in different directions. Fran danced a couple, but mainly sat with Jean, watching the mayhem with a huge smile on her face. The American couple, Marge and Brett were nowhere to be seen and Evie was surprised, knowing their sociable natures. She was not surprised that the enigmatic Arthur Ross had kept away.

Evie had helped a rather drunk Fran up the stairs to bed

well after midnight, and then had fallen into a deep, contented sleep. The next morning the sky was a brilliant bright blue and the mountains looked glorious through her window. Evie felt relaxed and optimistic as she pulled on her jeans and sweater, ran a brush through her brown hair and went to knock on Fran's door.

The dining room had been put back to normal for breakfast, although the floor was suspiciously sticky in a couple of places, and a new sense of community had taken hold. Rather than the hill walkers and the painters choosing separate tables, she now saw Kayleigh and Helen sitting with a couple of walkers and George and Jean on another table with two more. Evie couldn't for the life of her remember the walkers' names, but they called out a cheery 'hello' as she and Fran sat down nearby. Evie loaded her plate with sausage, black pudding and tattie scones, but Fran stuck to black coffee.

'Look at the weather!' enthused Evie, 'It's going to be brilliant today. I wonder if it's going to be rivers or waterfalls or sea this morning.'

In fact it was all about the sea. Aggie explained the different methods of isolating the white on the paper to make the crests of waves and sea spray, either by using wax, or masking fluid, or by cheating and adding a little gouache or acrylic to the finished painting. She demonstrated each one, and the group had a go, with varying degrees of success. Evie was excited about the afternoon plan. They were taking the minivan down to Elgol, the little fishing village on the shores of Loch Scavaig, said to be where Bonnie Prince Charlie had hidden in a cave. It sounded wild and romantic, and Evie couldn't wait.

But at lunch, a shadow of worry was cast over the day. Fran and Evie noticed the hotel manager, Mr Harris, going discreetly from table to table, asking questions with a solemn expression on his face. Guests were shaking their heads regretfully. Then the manager arrived at their table. He leaned towards them and said in a very quiet voice:

'We're a wee bit concerned about two of our guests. The chambermaid checked their room this morning, and their bed hadn't been slept in. It's Marjory and Brett Carter, from the USA. I don't suppose you know anything about their whereabouts yesterday?'

'Well, yes, we do, actually,' said Fran. 'We had lunch with them yesterday. They said they were doing a history trail in the afternoon and wanted to visit ruined castles and clearance villages.'

'OK, that's very helpful. Thank you.'

'There was another thing, another place they wanted to visit but I can't remember the word. It began with a 'b' I think,' Fran added.

'Could it be 'broch'?'

'Yes, that's it!'

'It's an iron-age circular tower. There are half a dozen on Skye.'

'And they were going to talk to Arthur Ross and ask him for suggestions where to go,' added Evie.

The manager rubbed his chin, thoughtfully. 'Arthur Ross, you say? He didn't mention that. Well, I'll go and see if I can track him down again. We're not sure they came back to the hotel yesterday evening. Their car isn't in the car park. They might have broken down somewhere. Well, thank you very much, ladies, and sorry to disturb your lunch.'

Evie and Fran looked at each other, concerned.

'You don't think it's anything to do with that feeling you had yesterday of being somewhere cold and dark?' asked Fran.

'I don't know. I'd forgotten all about that. I had such a nice day yesterday, I didn't even think about it. Do you think I should tell the manager?'

'Um, no, it's so hard to explain. And they probably did just run out of petrol or something.'

'But why didn't they phone?'

'I bet the reception is really bad in some places. I'm sure they'll turn up today.'

Evie closed her eyes and emptied her mind, trying to force the vision to come again, but there was nothing. She opened her eyes to find Fran giving her a knowing look.

'Hey,' said Fran, putting a hand on her arm, 'Don't worry about it. There's nothing you can do. They'll turn up safe and sound. Don't let it spoil your day; you were so excited about this afternoon.'

***

The drive that afternoon was even more beautiful than the last one. Roddy picked them up at two o'clock, and they set off towards the east coast this time, following the main road as it wound its way around the lochs and inlets to their left, with the barren greenish-brown hillsides rising up steeply to their right. The road was smooth and fast, despite the number of cars, and they made good time down to Broadford. On the outskirts of the town they turned onto a narrow single-track road. The houses gradually became fewer and fewer as the road climbed up into the bracken-covered hills. Here were the rounded peaks of the Red Cuillins, glowing gold and russet in the sunshine. Sheep loitered on the road and lazily moved to the side, their unshorn wool hanging in shreds from their sides. Flashes of bright yellow gorse contrasted sharply with the reds and golds of the hillsides, which were reflected in a small reed-filled loch. The traffic was light and they passed few cars. The main obstacles Roddy had to navigate were the complacent, ragged sheep, the narrow cattle-grids and groups of hill walkers with heavy backpacks. They passed the ruined church of Cill Chroisd on the right, the gravestones just visible behind a low stone wall, and Evie had a sudden memory of another ruined church. She shivered. But the views were too enchanting to dampen her spirits for long. The road twisted and turned along the eastern arm of Loch Slapin, and then turned to hug the north bank. Here the mountains cast a dark shadow over the road, but the loch shone an icy blue, with a streak of silver visible out towards the sea. Once past the little village of Torrin, they left the friendly, rounded Red Cuillins behind and were confronted by the towering mass of Blaven, the first, and supposedly the least dangerous, of the Black Cuillins. The road climbed up and up above the loch, then dropped down to the small fishing hamlet of Elgol. White-walled cottages were sprinkled over the hillsides. Fishing boats and tourist boats mingled in the small harbour. They parked in the little car park and carried their equipment down to the shore. Here the view was absolutely astonishing. In the foreground were the piled up rocks and pebbles of the beach, in all shades of blue, green, purple and brown. To the right, the high cliffs rose vertically up from the stony beach, scarred with horizontal indentations. The water in the bay shone a bright blue, but what took their breath away was the sight on the far side of the bay. They were looking into the very heart of a savage mountain-scape. The full horseshoe-shaped range of the Black Cuillins glowered back at them, magnificent, forbidding and powerful. This was a completely different perspective of the mountains from their view of two days ago, and much more dramatic. Evie felt dwarfed by the majesty, but at the same time could hardly wait to get her paints out.

The group struggled to find even ground for their camping chairs on the stony shore, but eventually all were seated and beginning to paint. A couple of tourists wandered among them to admire the work and to chat, but otherwise they were completely silent, lost in a world of colour. Aggie beamed as she went from person to person, gently encouraging and suggesting. Everyone produced good work that afternoon; it was almost impossible not to. Even George was happy. They folded their chairs away and gathered round Roddy for tea, coffee and scotch eggs.

'The tide's out,' said Roddy, looking over at Aggie. 'Does anyone fancy a walk to Bonnie Prince Charlie's cave?'

'Have we got time?' worried Aggie. 'We won't make it back to the hotel before seven.'

'It's only about a forty minute drive back in the van, so I reckon we could do it, if we're quick. Does anyone want to?'

Aggie put it to the vote: 'Well, what do you all say? Those who want to walk could walk, the others could get a hot cup of coffee at the café just up the hill. But we probably wouldn't get back in time to shower before dinner. It's up to you.'

It was decided to stay another hour or so at Elgol. Evie and Fran were delighted to get the chance to stretch their legs after sitting hunched over their watercolour blocks for the last couple of hours. Kayleigh decided to walk too, although Roddy was not sure her white fashion boots were appropriate for the terrain. And so Aggie took Jean, George and Helen for coffee, and the walkers set off after Roddy. He set a fast pace, and they scrambled to catch up over the boggy hillside, keeping away from the edge of the cliff and inching nervously past a group of lazy chestnut-brown cows. Then they dropped down through a cutting onto the shore. Here the rocks were slippery and treacherous, and Evie and Fran were glad of their hiking boots. Kayleigh slithered and swore, until Roddy doubled back to give her a helping hand. They hugged the cliffs along the shoreline, went past a first small cave, then came to a second cave, hidden behind boulders. The entrance was narrow and water dripped down from the ceiling. Inside, the rocks were incredible shades of blue, brown and purple with vibrant green ferns and mosses growing between the cracks.

'Is this really where Bonnie Prince Charlie stayed?' asked Evie.

'Well, there's caves all over Scotland where Bonnie Prince Charlie was supposed to have hidden, but it's pretty certain he did stay here, on his last night, before he fled to France. It goes back about fifty metres, but we've no time to explore today.' Roddy gestured around the cave, slowly and reverently, his eyes ablaze with passion. 'But just imagine for a moment, you're standing where he stood! Where he sat and ate his last meal on Scottish soil!'

He's so proud of his heritage, thought Evie. It's attractive. She could imagine him wielding a claymore as he charged into battle in defence of the Stuart pretender. 'So would you have been a Jacobite, back in the day?' she teased.

'Oh, aye, for sure! I'd have been fighting against you English invaders. Scotland for the Scottish!' He grinned, taking the edge off his words.

'Did you vote for independence then?'

'Aye, I did. Maybe it'll happen in my lifetime. I hope so. Right, ladies, we'd best be getting back before the tide turns. We don't want to be stuck here all night.'

They picked their way back along the boulder-strewn beach and across the grassy hill to the car park, where they found the others waiting by the minivan.

Once aboard, Fran asked Evie: 'You know your vision of cold and damp and stone walls, do you think it was the cave? Could have been just a premonition of the walk we just did?'

'Could be. But I'm not sure. I felt a kind of sadness too.'

'Well, old Charlie would have been sad to leave Scotland. Maybe you felt that.'

'Yes. Yes, maybe you're right. Maybe that's all it was.'

The group were tired but happy, and more than one of the seven passengers nodded off as Roddy drove them back to the hotel. The evening sunshine lit up the tops of the Red Cuillins a deep crimson as they sped along the narrow road. What a perfect day, thought Evie. Just perfect. She hadn't once thought about Jake, or her tiny flat, or the house she'd had to leave. She realised, with a shock, that she was happy. She leant her head against Fran's shoulder and let her eyelids fall.

***

They sensed a change of atmosphere immediately on entering the hotel reception. A heaviness hung in the air, and a kind of expectant stillness.

'Is there any news of the Americans?' George asked the young receptionist.

'I'm afraid not,' she replied. 'We've contacted the police and the mountain rescue teams. They've started a search, but there's nothing yet. They're going to keep searching in the morning.' She looked upset, and Evie wondered if it was she who had found the couple's room empty that morning.

The atmosphere was subdued over dinner, and also in the bar afterwards. Evie bought the drinks and as she turned to Fran, she noticed the quiet, closed-off-looking man, Arthur Ross, sitting alone at a corner table, as always with his laptop open. Evie stared at him, taking in every detail. He was handsome, she admitted, in a cold and contained way. He reminded her of the shadowy KGB operatives in spy films, unobtrusive, blending into the background, but with a certain aura of watchfulness. His hair was short and dark, his brow was broad and unwrinkled. But those eyes, they were strange, unreadable, dark abysses of emptiness. His long legs were encased in black jeans and his sweater was a dark olive green. He had very fine fingers, she noticed, as he tapped out something on his laptop. Long and slender. She remembered Marge saying 'that man gives me the creeps'. On impulse, she gestured to the table with her drink. 'Come on, Fran, let's go sit with Mr Friendly over there. I want to ask him some questions.'

She plonked herself down in an armchair opposite the man, with Fran following in her wake. He looked up briefly, annoyed, then went back to his typing.

'So, how's the book coming on?' asked Evie with forced cheerfulness.

'Good,' he muttered, without looking up.

Evie gritted her teeth. This man was impossible, but she wasn't finished with him yet. 'You know the American couple who are missing?' He looked up at last. 'They were going to ask you where to go yesterday.' He stared at her, unblinking. Evie continued: 'So did you talk to them before they left?'

'No, I did not.'

'They wanted to visit clearance villages and other historic stuff. I told them you're an expert on the clearances.' She smiled sweetly, but he did not return the smile.

'I didn't speak to them. I didn't see them.'

'Oh, that's a shame. I thought that might help the police narrow down the search. So, tell me more about this current book. What kind of legends are you writing about?'

'This chapter is called Ritual Human Sacrifice in Pagan Scotland,' he stated, baldly.

'Shit!' said Fran, before she could stop herself. 'So that's why you were so interested in the murder.'

Arthur Ross looked from one woman to the other, his eyes narrowed. 'I don't know what you're implying, but I don't like your tone of voice, either of you. If you've got an accusation to make, then make it!' Evie and Fran shrank back in their chairs under his angry glare.

'No, no, of course not,' stuttered Fran.

'Then if you'll excuse me, I need to find somewhere quiet to write.' He slammed the laptop shut with force and left the bar.

'Come on, Evie, spill the beans!' said Fran, once he had disappeared. 'What are you thinking?'

'He's interested in ritual sacrifice. He was here at the time of the murder. Marge didn't trust him, said he was creepy. He was eavesdropping on police interviews. He's definitely weird. When he snatched the paper out of my hands the other day, maybe it's because the article talked about police having definite leads.'

'You think he could be the killer? What about your flashes, what do they tell you about him?'

'Nothing. Absolutely nothing at all.'

C HAPTER EIGHT: THE FLAT

The news that Jake had replaced her already hit Evie like a punch to the stomach. How could he? So quickly? Before they'd even had chance to talk things through? Shock changed to confusion, bitterness, then to anger as she processed this new information. This changed everything. Jake didn't want her back, and she was going to have to grow up and face facts. Their story was over. She was just going to have to make some kind of life without him.

Staying with her parents was becoming more and more difficult. She loved them, but felt she'd regressed to the sulky teenager she used to be since living back in the childhood home. Their tender concern made her snappy, and she knew she was being unfair to them. She was ruining their retirement years, when they should have been free to go out, have fun, travel. She had to move out.

'Dad, can I have a word?' she said one day, watching her dad plant tomatoes in the garden. As he stooped to make a hole in the soil, she was shocked to see how thin his hair had become. He's getting old, she thought, her heart constricted.

'Of course, love, what is it?'

'I think I should start looking for a flat.'

Her dad looked crestfallen. 'There's no need for that, love, you can stay here as long as it takes to sort things out with Jake.'

'That's the problem. I think Jake's moved on already.'

'Has he? No, that can't be right. He wouldn't do that.'

'Becca at work told me he has a new girlfriend.'

'Bastard! Bloody bastard!' Her dad put down his trowel and

looked at her. Anger was making his hands tremble and his face was turning crimson. 'Well, what do you want to do?' he asked.

'I'd like to find a little flat. Nothing too expensive. But money's a bit tight. I'm still paying half the mortgage. Do you think you could help me out with the rent, and then when we sell the house I'll pay you back for everything?'

'Well yes, of course, if that's really what you want. We paid your rent while you were at university, so it'll be like the old days.'

'But you're both on a pension, I don't want you to have to struggle. I've seen little flats that look OK for about five hundred a month, would that be a stretch?'

'I'm sure we could manage that. But we don't want you to live anywhere grotty, or in a bad area. We'd rather see you somewhere decent and pay a bit more.'

And so Evie and her mum and dad started flat-hunting around the Wakefield area. It was actually almost enjoyable, and gave the three of them a project they could discuss without risk of upsetting each other. Evie's mother was in her element, discussing furnishings and fittings. Her dad was more practical, checking for loose plugs and draughty windows. They found a one-bed apartment in a converted hospital building. It was tiny, but clean and safe.

'This'll do fine' said Evie, and she phoned the agency to arrange to sign the lease.

'Don't you think you ought to tell Jake before you sign?' her mum had said. 'He might have had a change of heart. He might want to talk about this.'

'There's nothing to discuss really. I suppose I'll have to tell him I want some of the furniture from the house, eventually.'

That evening she wrote a terse email to Jake.

Becca says you're moving on with your life, so I'm going to move on too. I'm renting a flat in Wakefield. These are the items of furniture I'd like: the spare room bed and wardrobe, the small kitchen table, the reclining chair, pots, pans, casserole dishes and cutlery, duvet and sheets. Please can you get everything ready, and I'll come and collect one day when you're at work. Everything else we can talk about once we've got the house on the market. Evie.

She received a phone call the next morning.

'What the fuck, Evie, what the fuck? Again you've gone off and done your own thing without talking to me!'

'But you haven't made any effort to talk to me either!'

'You want us to sell the house? Really? Is this what you want?'

'I don't see much alternative. I hear from Becca that you've got a new girlfriend.'

'What? No, I ...'

'It's OK. We're finished. You can do what the hell you like.' She put the phone down, feeling quite satisfied that she'd had the last word.

*****

A few weeks later, Evie was unpacking boxes in her flat and trying to convince herself that small was sustainable and easy to manage. She'd married young, too young maybe. Lots of her friends were still single. There was still time to start again, to have a family. But the thought of dating again filled her with dread. She slashed the tape on another box with her cutter and reached inside. She took out some of the books that Jake had decided were hers. Then she unwrapped a rectangular object wrapped in newspaper. There was her wedding photo. There was Jake, looking solid and dependable in his grey morning suit. And there she was, in her simple sheath dress, her brown hair caught up in a twist and studded with seed pearls. They looked so happy. And it was all so recent. Shockingly recent. How had it all turned to shit so fast? Evie replaced the photo frame in the box and went to pour herself a large glass of wine. She sat in the single armchair, let the tears fall and indulged in a good cry.

Later that afternoon the intercom buzzed. Evie pressed the button and heard a female voice say: 'Delivery for Mrs Carpenter.' She buzzed the main entrance open, expecting an Amazon delivery of two lampshades. A few moments later there was a knock on her door. Evie opened it, and there stood her sister.

'Fran! Oh, Fran, am I glad to see you!' She threw herself at her sister and they hugged tightly. Tears came back into her eyes, but this time tears of gratitude.

'Well, let's have a look at this flat of yours,' said Fran, untangling herself. She wandered round the living room-kitchen and poked her head round the bedroom door. 'It's nice, she declared. 'Very neat and fresh. Good for a new start.'

'I don't know if I can do it, Fran', said Evie. 'I feel like a total failure, I've lost all my confidence. I can barely bring myself to leave the flat in the evening. I just sit and mope and watch awful TV. Tripey channel five movies. And they make me cry!'

'You'll get there,' said Fran. 'It takes time. But listen. I've booked us a holiday. I've got time owing, and I'm sure you can get compassionate leave if you don't have any holiday left. We're going to go away together, just you and me.'

'You can't do that, you work so hard! You should save your holidays for something really special. You don't want to mope around with me.'

'No arguing. It's all booked and paid for. We are going on a ten-day painting holiday on the Isle of Skye!'

'Fran, it's a lovely idea but I don't think I can. I haven't really got the finances for...'

'Oh shut up, you daft cow. There's got to be some advantage to having an obscenely well-paid job in London and living the single life. This is what I want to do. So stop arguing. I'm picking you up in two weeks. All you need are your clothes and watercolour paints. Now, pour me a drink and tell me all about your plans for this flat!'

CHAPTER NINE: WAITING

Everyone's nerves were on edge the next morning. The atmosphere at breakfast was gloomy. No-one spoke much. Evie couldn't face her normal full Scottish breakfast, and managed a mere piece of toast with her cup of tea.

The sisters walked to the art room feeling reluctant. It seemed disrespectful, cavalier even, to paint when two people were missing somewhere on the island. They pushed the door open and found the rest of the group standing around Aggie, not sitting at the tables as they usually did.

'Great, you're here,' said Aggie. 'We were just talking about what to do today. I think we're all feeling a bit jangly, but I'm not sure it's a good idea to sit around waiting for news. I think we should go out this morning, what do you think?'

There were murmurs of agreement.

'Where should we go?' asked George.

'Here's what I thought. We could ask the hotel to make up some sandwiches, then head off to the north west coast. We could stop at Neist Point, if it's not too busy. The view is amazing there; it's a steep ridge of cliffs leading to a lighthouse. You can see the Outer Hebrides on a good day; the weather looks mixed today, but we might be lucky. Plus there's a chance of seeing whales. We could do some sketching there. And we could come back via Dunvegan Castle, maybe sketch there too, if there's time. It's one of Scotland's oldest castles and has beautiful gardens. We'd be back by mid-afternoon. How does that sound?'

And so it was agreed. Aggie went off to organise some food and to find Roddy, while the others went to fetch outdoor clothes. Half an hour later, they were waiting outside the hotel entrance when Roddy pulled up in the minivan. He seemed less than enthusiastic about the plan.

'Neist Point, Aggie, are you sure? That's high up on the tourist agenda. It'll be hoaching!'

'Well, we'll give it a try. We can always turn back if it's too busy.'

Roddy shook his head and sighed, and climbed into the driving seat. He's not helping us into the minivan today, thought Evie. He must be in a bad mood.

The drive was torturous. Once they'd left the main road on the outskirts of Dunvegan, the road was the narrowest they'd yet encountered. They drove over an undulating grassy plain with many blind summits. Pretty whitewashed cottages dotted the hillsides. Over the brows of hills they frequently found sheep in the middle of the road, and Roddy waited patiently for them to wander off idly to the verges. A constant stream of cars came in the opposite direction, but passing places were luckily fairly frequent. A light rain began to fall and the sky darkened. When they passed the village of Glendale, the road became shockingly narrow and rough. Roddy swore as he navigated between the traffic and the potholes. Then, finally, at the highest point, they were confronted by mayhem. Cars and camper vans were parked along both sides of the road on the soft, muddy verges. Many of the vans were stuck. Wheels were spinning as drivers tried to get some purchase on the sodden ground. Oncoming cars waited ahead while other cars attempted to three-point turn between the vans. Drivers had left their vehicles and were standing in the rain, gesticulating angrily.

'Fuck this, Aggie!' swore Roddy. 'We're not even at the car park yet and it's full. I'm going to try to turn back while we still can!'

'Sorry, Roddy. You were right. This is madness.' Aggie looked crestfallen. 'We should never have come here.'

Roddy managed to reverse back far enough to execute an eight-point turn, and they set off, back the way they'd come. All that way, for nothing, thought Evie. What a waste of time. This feels like it's going to be a shit day. She stared out of the windows at a landscape which had turned bleak and dull in the rain.

'So, where should we head to now?' Roddy asked Aggie.

'I don't know. If it's so busy here, Dunvegan Castle is going to be stowed out too.' For the first time, Aggie seemed unsure of herself. She ran a hand through her mop of curly grey hair. 'What do you suggest?'

'I've got an idea. A nice view, dead quiet, and I guarantee not one fucking camper van.'

It took another hour before they reached their destination. Eventually Roddy parked up in the tiny hamlet of Uignish. It consisted of a couple of farm buildings beside a narrow loch, and little else. Evie wondered why they had come here. Wearily, they got out, picked up a camping chair each and followed Roddy up a grassy bank. The rain had stopped and a tentative sun peeped out from behind the clouds. At the top of the bank, Roddy turned to them and said: 'Here you are. Best view on Skye and nae bugger here!' He pointed out over the loch. It was a gentle view, but stunning. The wonderful contrast of colours made Evie tingle with anticipation. The vivid green of the grassy hill dipped down into the bright orange-yellow of late-flowering gorse bushes at the loch side, then the deep blue of the water. Beyond that, on the other shore, was the olive green of mature woodland, and standing proudly amongst the trees, Dunvegan castle, in all its baronial glory of pepper-pot turrets and battlements. Behind the castle keep, with it's square tower and flagpole, was a line of darker green fir trees, and further beyond that the low mountains shone purple as the sun touched the heather. Above it all, a pale blue sky.

'Well done, Roddy. This is just the job,' said Aggie, setting up her chair on the crest of the hill. She turned to the group, once more the confident teacher, in full command. 'Now, there are one or two important things to consider when you tackle a panorama like this. Composition is key! Don't try and cram everything in. Think about what you want your focal point to be, and place that off-centre. Don't fall into the trap of putting the castle bang in the middle of your picture. You might want to make your focal point the gorse, for example, and have everything else recede back into the distance. I suggest you take a piece of rough paper, divide it into four and figure out four different layouts, some portrait orientation and some landscape. See what grabs the most interest.'

The time passed quickly for Evie. She finished her painting well before the others and was pleased with it. She'd captured the castle in a few soft brushstrokes, but mainly concentrated on the wonderful play of rainbow colours. She put down her paper and brushes and sighed contentedly. She stood up to stretch her back and threw her arms wide. She closed her eyes for a moment and took a deep breath of refreshing salty sea air. A shadow passed over her. It was Roddy, holding out a cup of tea.

'I thought you might need a wee drink before lunch,' he said.

'Oh, thanks, lovely.'

To her surprise, he sat down on the grass and gestured for her to join him.

'The grass is quite dry now,' he said. 'I was watching you painting just now, from just above. Your painting looked really good. Would it be ok to show it to me?' he asked, almost shyly.

'Yes, of course.' Evie turned over the cover of the painting block and handed it to Roddy. He took his time, his eyes darting between the painting and the landscape before them.

'I love it,' he said. He touched the paper, lovingly, reverently.

'Is this place special to you?' Evie asked.

'Oh aye. Very special. I was born here. Well, just down the road. A wee hamlet called Heribost.'

'Really? Is it pretty?'

'It is. It used to be a good little community too, but it's mostly just holiday lets now.'

On impulse Evie said: 'You're welcome to keep the painting, if you'd like to?'

'Really? Are you sure?' She nodded. 'Thank you! I'll get it framed and hang it in my house. Thank you.'

They sat in silence for a few moments, enjoying the view. A couple of sailing boats were making their way down the loch towards the sea. Sheep bleated in the distance.

'Is this your first time on Skye?' Roddy asked.

'Yes. It's so beautiful it breaks your heart. I've seen mountains before. I went to the Swiss Alps and to the Dolomites when I was younger with my parents, but this is something else. It's hard to put into words. It's magical.'

Roddy turned his head and smiled at her. Their eyes met and Evie saw that his irises were the colour of liquid honey. She turned her head quickly and looked into her tea mug, mortified to have felt a little tug of desire.

'Where do you live, then?' asked Roddy.

'Wakefield, in Yorkshire.'

'Is that pretty?'

'No! Not at all! But you can get out into the countryside pretty easily. The Dales are beautiful.'

'I see you're married,' Roddy said, pointing at her ring finger. She still wore the simple gold band. 'Did your man not want to come to Skye with you?'

Evie surprised herself by replying easily, with no particular sadness: 'We're separated. And he would have hated all this art talk. He's the practical type, not at all arty.'

Roddy glanced at her, then down at his feet. He mumbled: 'The man must be a right numpty to let you slip through his fingers.' Evie started. Then, as if embarrassed to have spoken his thoughts aloud, Roddy sprang to his feet. 'Right then, I'd best be getting the picnic out the van. You all must be starving!'

Evie's eyes followed him as he strode down the hill. She wasn't sure she'd heard properly. And what on earth was a 'numpty'? She was pretty sure she'd been paid a nice compliment though. It felt good. She looked back at the group of painters and saw Kayleigh looking back at her with a quizzical expression. Evie smiled and gave a slight shake of her head, indicating that she had no interest in Roddy. But then she checked herself. Was that true? There was something about him. She'd seen something soft and vulnerable just now that had stirred an emotional reaction in her. Maybe moving on from Jake was not going to be impossible after all, she thought.

The group ate a picnic of ham sandwiches, scotch pies and crisps, enjoying the sunshine and chatting. After the remains were once again packed away in the minivan, Aggie asked the group what they wanted to do next.

'Does anyone want to stay a bit longer to finish up? Jean, George, Fran, you've not finished yet. Shall we give it another hour maybe? And are the rest of you ok to hang around a bit longer here?'

'Yes, no problem,' said Evie. 'It's beautiful here, really peaceful.' She turned to Helen and Kayleigh. 'Come on, there's a gap in the gorse over there. Let's walk down to the shore and explore.'

The three women picked their way over the rough grass, past the prickly gorse and onto the shore. Clumps of slippery orange seaweed littered the ground and they saw shells and bright sea glass. Tiny crabs scuttled for cover in rockpools. The air was fresh and briny. Gulls screeched overhead.

'They'll have to paint us into their pictures,' Evie joked, looking back towards the three painters on the hill above. Idly she picked up a flattish stone and crouched to skim it onto the water. Three bounces, then it disappeared. To her surprise,

Helen picked a stone and did the same. Five skips before sinking.

'Show me how you do that!' said Kayleigh.

'Pick a flat stone and curl your finger round it like this,' said Helen, choosing a small flat stone and demonstrating. 'Then throw it as hard as you can, quite low to the water.' She flung the stone expertly and it skipped across the loch in a series of rapidly diminishing bounces.

'Wow,' said Evie, 'that was seven at least!'

Helen found a second flat stone and handed it to Kayleigh, who managed two skips. The three women spent several minutes engrossed in skimming, until Roddy ran down to join them at the shoreline. He rolled up the sleeves of his old fisherman's sweater, put his hands on his hips and said: 'Right ladies, let me show you how this is done!' The four of them competed happily for a few more minutes, until Evie turned to Helen and asked:

'Do you fancy walking along the shoreline a bit?'

'Yes, OK,' said Helen with a knowing smile, and they started to pick their way along the peninsula towards the sea. When they were a little distance from the others, Helen asked: 'Did you want to give those two some time together?'

'How did you guess?' asked Evie, with a grin.

'It's obvious she likes him,' replied Helen. 'But I'm not sure it's mutual. I think our Roddy has a bit of a soft spot for you!'

'Oh, I'm not sure about that,' said Evie, blushing, keeping her eyes on the ground. She couldn't help feeling a little bit pleased though. Maybe he does like me! Do I like him? Well... maybe... Despite the heartache of her separation from Jake, she had to admit that she did. She knew it was more of a sexual attraction than a meeting of minds. They had little in common, apart from a respect for the landscape. But she could easily imagine herself pressed up against that old sweater, with his broad arms encircling her. She wondered if he was a good kisser. At times he seemed almost innocent, maybe inexperienced. She shook her head to dispel these thoughts, and to change the subject, she asked:

'Are you finding the painting therapeutic? Is it what you hoped it would be? You're making fantastic progress!'

'Thanks. I am enjoying it actually. I'm surprising myself. There are moments when I even manage to forget what a nightmare the last two years have been.'

'Were you married a long time? I'm sorry, maybe you don't want to talk about it…'

'No, no, I absolutely do. I hate it when people think they have to avoid talking about my husband Geoff. It's like he's being erased bit by bit. We were married almost thirty years. He got pancreatic cancer.'

'That's shit. I'm so sorry. What was he like?'

'Oh, just a lovely man. A keen gardener, a cricket fan, a lover of crosswords and puzzles. Very gentle, very kind.'

'He sounds great. You were lucky to have a good marriage.'

'Yes, yes, we were.' Helen smiled, then gave Evie a searching look. 'What about you? You're married aren't you?' She glanced down at Evie's left hand. 'But I gather this year hasn't been easy for you either?'

'No, it's been pretty awful. We split up, my husband Jake and I. I did something he said he couldn't forgive.' Evie glanced up at Helen and saw that the older woman was looking uncomfortable. 'No, no, not an affair. Nothing like that. I went away for a week and lied to him about where I was going because I knew he wouldn't approve. He said he couldn't trust me any more after that.'

Helen stopped walking and laid a hand on Evie's arm. 'Marriage is never simple. There are so many ups and downs. We had quite a few, believe me. But that sounds like something you should both be able to work through.'

'That's what I thought too. But I found out he's got a new

girlfriend.'

'Oh dear.' Helen sighed, then her face brightened. 'Well, in that case, maybe he wasn't the right man for you after all. Plenty more fish…'

The two women turned to walk back towards the group, then Evie stopped, put a hand on Helen's shoulder and whispered: 'Look!'

They were being watched. Just a few short metres away, in the still sea loch, a head had emerged. Two large, round, black eyes stared straight back at them, inquisitive, watchful. The seal's head was a mottled grey, sleek and shiny, its body suspended, motionless, in the water, small ripples spreading out around it. There was a moment of complete silence, then the beautiful creature slipped below the water, leaving just the ring of ripples.

Helen and Evie let out the breath they had unconsciously been holding and grinned at each other. 'That was special,' said Helen. 'That was just for us. It means we're both going to be OK!' She linked an arm through Evie's and together they made their way back to the others.

They found the group hurriedly packing away their painting things and folding up the camping chairs, but they were aware at once of a change in atmosphere.

'What's up?' Evie asked Fran. 'Has something happened?'

'Yes, Aggie got a phone call. We're needed back at the hotel. They've found Marge and Brett.'

'Are they… are they dead?'

'Aggie wouldn't say. She just said we need to go now. The police want to speak to us.'

'Oh God. That sounds bad.'

'Yes. It doesn't sound good.'

C HAPTER TEN: QUESTIONS

Roddy drove fast once they were back on the main road south. No-one talked very much as the minivan sped back towards the Old Manse. They arrived just after half past three in the afternoon. Mr Harris, the hotel manager, walked down the steps to meet them as they filed out of the minibus.

'This is such dreadful news,' he said, his hand raking through his sparse hair and his brows knitted with worry. 'So distressing. The police are here. They've talked to the staff and most of the other guests already, but they'd like to talk to all of you too. I've got tea and coffee and biscuits set out in the bar. If you'd like to dump your things, then go straight to the bar, the detectives will call you in from there.'

'What's happened to the American couple, did they tell you?' asked George.

'They found the bodies late this morning. That's all I can say, really, I'm sorry. I'll have to leave the rest to the police.'

'Do they want to talk to me and Roddy too?' asked Aggie. 'I don't think I ever met the couple.'

'Yes, I believe so.'

Ten minutes later, the solemn group gathered in the bar. Roddy served the tea and coffee, and they began to talk quietly.

'Why do you think the police want to talk to us?' asked Kayleigh. 'Surely they just had an accident or something.'

'It must be something more serious, I think,' replied George. 'Maybe a joint suicide pact? Or maybe murder.'

'Not suicide,' said Fran. 'They were far too happy for that.

They had such plans, they had a whole bunch of Speyside distilleries to visit next week.'

'So... murder?' whispered Kayleigh.

'Let's not speculate,' said Aggie. 'We'll find out soon enough.'

Fran took her coffee and sat down next to Evie. 'What do you think?' she asked quietly. 'Any insight?'

'It's bad. That feeling of sadness, cold, damp stone walls, it came to me again.'

'But nothing new?'

'No.'

Before they could talk any further, a young uniformed policeman entered the bar.

'Francesca Lloyd please, could you come this way?' he asked in a soft Highland accent.

Fran put her coffee cup down and briefly squeezed Evie's shoulder. 'Back in a bit,' she said with a determined look.

Twenty minutes later, Fran reappeared with the young policeman. 'Your turn, sis!' she said to Evie, giving her a bright, encouraging smile. Evie rose and followed the policeman down the corridor and into one of the smaller conference rooms in the new wing. Two plain-clothes police officers were sitting at one side of a round table. They gestured for her to take a seat opposite.

'My name is Sergeant Reid, I'm from Portree Police, and this is Detective Sergeant Sterling from the Major Investigations Team in Inverness.' Sergeant Reid was in his late fifties, Evie estimated, with a kindly, craggy face and a soft Highland burr. The second detective was altogether different: younger, sharp-suited, urban and serious with a narrow face, thin lips and calculating eyes.

'Could you confirm your name please?'

'Evelyn Charlotte Carpenter, née Lloyd.'

'And your address?'

'Flat six, 1 A Oak Court, Pinderfields Road, Wakefield.'

'Thank you. We'd like to ask you some questions about the last movements of Marjory and Brett Carter. I understand you and your sister were just about the last people to speak to them before they disappeared.'

'Yes,' said Evie, starting to relax under the gentle gaze of the older man. 'We had lunch with them the day before yesterday and they told us their plans for the afternoon.'

'Can you tell me what they said, and if possible, use their exact words?'

'Um, I'm not sure about the exact words, but Brett said they wanted a change from whisky. He said his ancestors had come over from Scotland in the clearances, and they wanted to do some history visits. They mentioned clearance villages, castles and brochs.'

'OK. Anything else?'

'We told them to speak to Arthur Ross, a guest here. He wrote a book about the clearances in Skye.'

'Do you know if they did speak to Mr Ross?'

'No, sorry, I don't.'

'What else did you talk about?'

'Um, a bit about American politics, Donald Trump, um… I'm sorry, I can't remember much else. They left while we were still finishing our lunch.'

'And how did they seem to you? What was their state of mind?'

'Um…positive. Enthusiastic. They were both very open, very chatty people. Talkative, inquisitive, like Americans sometimes are.'

'Did you see them again after you finished your lunch?'

'No. I remember thinking it was strange they weren't at the ceilidh that night. They were very sociable.'

'Can you think of anything else that might be useful?'

Evie hesitated, not knowing whether to continue with what might just be hearsay. The younger detective, DS Sterling, leant forward in his seat, his posture noticeably more impassive and clinical than the local officer.

'Come on! Spit it out!' he snapped, making Evie jump.

'OK. This might be nothing. But Marge said she didn't like Arthur Ross. She said he was creepy. She was about to tell us something else but Brett told her not to gossip.'

The two detectives looked at each other, and Sergeant Reid made a note in his book. There was a moment of silence.

'Can I ask what happened to them?' asked Evie at last.

'We found their bodies just before noon today. They were lying inside the Dun Carloway broch.'

Evie swallowed. Cold, damp, rounded stone walls. 'How did they die?' she asked in a whisper.

'I am sorry to tell you, they were murdered,' said Sergeant Reid, softly.

'Were they... were they... did they have their clothes on?'

The older officer looked at her strangely for a moment. 'They were partially clothed. Their shoes had been removed.'

'And...um... did they have their arms crossed over their chests?'

This time both officers started visibly. Both sat a little straighter in their chairs. The pen was frozen in mid-gesture in Sergeant Reid's hand. There was a beat. Then the two men looked at each other. Some form of silent communication passed between them.

'Why do you ask that?' asked the younger man, unsmiling.

'Well, because of that girl before. The French influencer girl.'

'What do you know about her?'

'Well, she was found in an old churchyard, wasn't she? Naked, with her arms crossed over her chest.'

The younger detective leant forward again. His icy blue eyes bored into hers for a long moment. Evie started to squirm in her chair, aware that she had aroused their suspicion somehow.

'What makes you say the arms were crossed over the chest?'

'Well it was… um…' She dried up.

'That detail was never released to the public. So I ask again, how did you know that the girl's arms were crossed?' This time the detective's voice was distinctly cold. He stared at her with unblinking eyes.

Evie was at a loss. 'I…um…' she stuttered. She couldn't tell them about the visions could she? They would never believe her. The seconds ticked by and Evie remained silent.

'Where were you on the twenty-fifth of July of this year?' barked DS Sterling.

'Oh, you can't think…oh!' gasped Evie. 'I was at work, in Leeds.'

'Can you prove that?'

'Yes of course! You can ask my boss! Mr Thorpe in the Leeds Council Tourism department. I can give you the number!' she searched frantically in her pocket for her mobile phone.

'It's OK, no need to panic,' said Sergeant Reid, putting out a calming hand. 'We'll find the number if we need to check,' he continued in a gentler tone. 'Just tell us how you knew about the arms. Who did you talk to?'

Evie let out a sigh. She had no choice now. She would have to tell them. 'OK,' she started, 'I didn't talk to anyone. I just knew. Ever since I was a little girl I've had premonitions.' She glanced at them in turn, assessing their openness to what she was saying. 'You can check with my sister. She'll tell you this happens to me a lot.'

'Go on.'

'Well, on the first night we arrived here I had a kind of vision. I saw what I think was the murder scene.'

Sergeant Reid took up his pen once more. 'Tell us exactly what you saw in your vision,' he said.

'It was night. There was a fine crescent moon. It was a ruined church. There were gravestones. And the girl was lying on a sort of flat gravestone on the ground.'

'Go on,' he said again.

'She was naked and kind of posed, very straight and symmetrical. Her hair was brushed out behind her head. The arms were crossed like this.' She demonstrated on her own body. 'And she had bright red toenail polish.'

'Interesting,' conceded the older man.

'You don't think I'm nuts then?'

'Well, I have heard of psychics in the past who have helped solve murders, so I'll keep an open mind. You sure about the nail polish?' asked Sergeant Reid.

'Um, yes, pretty sure.'

'That's one detail that doesn't fit. The rest is pretty accurate. And did you experience any vision about Mr and Mrs Carter?'

'Yes,' said Evie cautiously. She wondered if he was humouring her, or if he really was interested. 'I felt an intense sadness, and being surrounded by cold, wet stone walls. Curved walls. I thought it was an old railway tunnel or something. That's all.'

'A broch has a double set of curved walls. They were found between the two walls,' said Sergeant Reid. The second detective gave him a sharp look, his eyes narrowed. Evie got the impression he hadn't believed a word of what she'd said.

'So we have a killer on the loose, and three victims,' said Sergeant Reid. 'What can you tell us to help catch the person who did this? Anything? Anything at all?'

'Just one thing,' replied Evie. 'You should talk to Arthur Ross. He knew about the arms being crossed too. He said the way the body was posed was ritualistic, and reminded him of Pagan rites or something. How would he have known that?'

'How indeed?' asked the older man. 'Well, I think that's all we need to know for now. Thank you for your time and please get in contact if you think of anything else that might be important.' He handed her his card and rose, signalling that the interview was over. The young uniformed officer, who had been lurking unobtrusively at the back of the room, came forward and opened the door, beckoning Evie to follow. As the door began to close behind them, Evie heard DS Sterling expel air through his mouth with a contemptuous 'pah!' and say 'Well that was a load of bull...' The rest was lost as the heavy door shut with a clunk.

Fran was waiting for Evie in the reception area. 'Do you want to go back to the bar with the others?' she asked.

'No, not really. I feel absolutely shattered. I just want to go and lie down for a bit.'

'Me too,' said Fran. 'I think I've got a headache coming on. I need to take an aspirin.'

'Is it one of your migraines?' asked Evie, worried. Fran was plagued by cluster headaches - violent migraines that came on with no warning, often years apart, but which could sometimes last for several days and were completely debilitating. They mostly struck late evening or at night, and left Fran in agony.

'Bloody well hope not!' said Fran, with forced cheerfulness. The two women climbed the stairs to the first floor. 'I'll feel better after a nap. Give me a knock when it's time to go down for dinner.'

***

In fact, both sisters overslept and were late down to dinner.

They found the dining room almost empty. The young waitress came up to their table with a worried expression. 'Och, I'm sorry, there's no more fish, I'm afraid, it's all away; there's just the beef stew left. Would that be OK? Or I could get cook to make an omelette?'

'An omelette would be absolutely perfect for me,' said Fran.

'And for me too,' said Evie. She had very little appetite. 'That would be wonderful. And a glass of white wine for me. What about you Fran?'

'Better not. Just water for me thanks.'

'How's your headache?' asked Evie, as the waitress went back to the kitchen with their order.

'Um, I think I'm keeping it at bay.'

'Let's have a look at your eyes.' Evie knew the warning signs of the cluster headaches. One of Fran's eyes would become bloodshot in the corner. She stared into her sister's eyes, concerned. 'Hmm, seems OK at the moment. Fingers crossed it's just regular headaches.'

The waitress returned with their drinks and two large omelettes with salad. 'It's cheese and ham. I forgot to ask if that's OK for yous? Ma heid's full o' mince just noo,' she said, slipping into a broad Scottish dialect. She looked about as tired as they felt.

'It's absolutely fine!' said Evie. 'Delicious.'

In fact Fran only managed half of her dinner. She put her knife and fork down, drank the rest of her water and said:

'Sorry, Evie, I am feeling a bit rough. A bit queasy. I'm going to go and lie down again. You stay and finish your dinner.'

'Shall I walk upstairs with you?'

'No, no, I'll be fine. Finish your meal and enjoy your wine. I'll be right as rain in the morning.' She got up from the table and walked, a little unsteadily, to the door.

Evie finished her omelette quickly. She didn't want to

linger in the deserted dining room. The floor-to-ceiling glass walls, so glorious in daylight, now showed nothing but the pitch darkness outside, and she felt horribly exposed under the bright central chandelier. For the first time she felt a tinge of fear. Three murders in the space of two short weeks. And all centred around this hotel. She gulped down the last of the wine, wiped her lips on the napkin and left the room. She hurried past the reception and started to climb the stairs, head down, suddenly desperate to be back in her room. She was about to fling open the fire door that lead to the first floor corridor when it suddenly opened. Evie reeled back a pace with a small gasp. Arther Ross stood barring her way, his face impassive. He took a step towards her, and she took a step back, now dangerously close to the edge of the stairs. He gave a small sardonic smile.

'Are you scared of me?' he asked.

'No, not at all,' Evie managed, looking him in the eye.

'Well, maybe you should be. After all, you think I'm a murderer don't you?'

'N-no.'

'You've been a little tittle-tattle haven't you? A snitch. Telling the police all kinds of stories about me.' He took another step towards her and Evie found herself teetering close to the top step, the stairs falling away behind her. She grabbed the handrail to steady herself. Arthur Ross came closer still, until his face was inches away from hers. Evie was mesmerised by his eyes. So black, so empty. It was like staring at someone wearing a mask, except there was no mask. Just blank, void spheres of emptiness. Evie felt she should scream, but was frozen to the spot.

'You'd better watch yourself,' he said, 'and start minding your own business. We don't want any more accidents, do we?' Once again he gave that chilling small smile, before pushing past her and running down the stairs. Evie started to tremble. She sat down heavily on the top step and held a hand to her chest.

Her heart was beating much too fast and she fought to control her breathing. She listened for footsteps, but could hear nothing. He'd gone. Unsteadily she got to her feet, opened the fire door and ran to her room, locking the door behind her. She leant against the door and took several deep breaths, releasing the air slowly, forcing herself to calm down.

Arther Ross, she thought. Was he messing with her? Was he just annoyed and vindictive that she'd talked about him to the police? Was he just a nasty little man, who enjoyed his moment of power, got off on seeing her scared? Or had that been some kind of confession? Was he the killer? Doing some kind of sick reenactment of Druid sacrificial rites? She wondered if the two police officers had taken her seriously. Had they maybe taken his fingerprints or done a DNA test? Evie was desperate to talk to Fran, but knew she should wait until morning. She undressed, had a shower and got into bed.

Sleep took a long time to come that night.

CHAPTER ELEVEN: STAY OR GO?

'Did you get a migraine last night?' asked Evie at breakfast.

'I did, but it wasn't the worst. It only lasted about half an hour.'

'You should have called me, I'd have come and pressed cold flannels to your forehead.' Evie had done this many times before, and it seemed to help.

'Honestly, it's easier being alone. I can't bear any noise or light. I just lie still and wait for it to pass. It always does in the end.'

'Poor you, it must be such a pain.'

'It is, but they only come every four or five years. It could be worse.'

'What brings them on, do you think?'

'No idea. Stress maybe? Yesterday's news was pretty horrific. Anyway, what about you? You look like you didn't get much sleep either.' Fran regarded Evie's face critically. She had shadows under her eyes and her skin was pale. Her dark brown hair was lank and lifeless.

'I didn't. I had a run in with that man, Arthur Ross.'

'Christ, did you? What happened?'

Evie looked around the dining room, making sure he was not there, and assessing if any others were within earshot. The room was strangely quiet and Evie wondered if some guests had left the hotel.

'I bumped into him at the top of the stairs,' she said, 'and I jumped a mile. He asked me if I was scared of him, and I said 'no'.

Then he said I should be scared, and he kind of implied that he could be the killer.'

'Did he say that in so many words?'

'Not exactly, but he warned me off talking to the police about him. Said there could be another accident.'

'Shit! What a creep! But was he just being an arse? I mean, if he is the killer he'd be stupid to admit it.'

'I don't know, I can't decide. He is rude, aggressive, solitary, but does that make him a suspect? On the other hand things are starting to add up: the eavesdropping, his interest in pagan sacrifice, and especially the fact that he knew about the victims' arms being crossed.'

'What do you mean? What's special about the arms?'

'I told the detectives about my vision yesterday. I had to, because I thought they were starting to suspect me; I'd asked if Marge and Brett's arms had been crossed like the French girl's. They looked at me really strangely and said that that information had never been released to the public. So how the hell did Arthur Ross know about it?'

'True. That's weird. But then, why would he talk about it openly to us in the bar?'

'I don't know! I'm confused as hell. I'm going to try and find out more about him on Google.'

'OK, good idea. But we should be careful now. Don't go around on your own any more. We'll stick together at all times.' Fran looked about the room, taking in the empty tables. 'It looks as if some people have packed up and left, unless they just ate breakfast really early. The walkers are here, and George, and that couple from Germany, but I can't see anyone else. What do you want to do? Do you think we should leave too?'

'Well, the police didn't stop us from leaving, so we could do, in theory. But I'd prefer to stay, if that's OK with you. I still feel like I'm meant to stay, for some reason.'

'It's up to you. We have got three more days of the art workshop to do, if that's still going ahead. Or maybe they'll have cancelled it?'

'I don't know. We'll see what happens at ten o'clock, I guess.' Evie turned to look at the view. Rain spattered in machine-gun bursts against the tall windows and the mountains had disappeared under ominous clouds. 'The weather's crap today, so I doubt we'll be going out anywhere.'

'I phoned mum and dad this morning,' said Fran, a little sheepishly. 'I tried to downplay things as much as I could, just said that a couple had been found dead in strange circumstances and implied that we thought it was kind of exciting to be interviewed by the police. But they were horrified, as you can imagine. They begged us to pack up and leave today.'

'Oh dear. Mum always goes overboard. I'm bound to get a phone call too, then. Listen, I don't want to push you into staying if you'd rather go?'

Fran was about to answer when the dining room door opened and Kayleigh walked in, looked around, and spotted them. She was immaculately dressed in tan trousers, her usual white boots and beige cashmere jumper. Not a blonde hair was out of place. Her eyebrows had been expertly pencilled in and her lips outlined in dark pink. She walked over to their table and sat on the edge of a seat.

'Hi! I'm glad I found you. I just wanted to say goodbye. I'm not staying.'

'Oh, that's a shame!' said Evie. 'Are you sure?'

'Yeah, well,' said Kayleigh, 'my art is crap and now with a fucking murderer on the loose, I mean, why would anyone stay?'

'I think we'll stick it out,' said Fran. 'There's only three more days and we're safe if we stick together.'

'How are you getting back?' asked Evie. 'You live in London, don't you?'

'Dunno yet. I'll probably get a taxi to Kyle and then get a

train. I haven't figured that out yet. Anyway, I'd better go and pack.' She rose from the chair, and on impulse Evie did the same, edged round the table and gave Kayleigh a brief hug.

'It was really nice to meet you,' she said. 'Look at you, you look like a film star. You've got everything going for you; you'll get there. You just need to find out what you love doing.'

'Not effing watercolours, that's for sure!' said Kayleigh with a short laugh.

'Don't be so hard on yourself. I liked your stuff. There's nothing prim or tentative about them; you just totally go for it. You have a great life, you hear?'

Kayleigh returned the hug. 'Thanks. And you two enjoy your last three days. Think of me in London having a massive retail therapy splurge when you're out there painting in the miserable cold. Oh my God, I can hardly wait.' She left the dining room with a cheery backwards wave.

Fran pulled a face at Evie. 'That was a bit OTT, wasn't it?' she said, amused. 'What's with the agony aunt stuff?'

'I like her,' said Evie. 'She's a lost soul. All the gear and no idea. Hope she'll be OK.' For some reason Evie felt almost maternal towards Kayleigh, an urge to protect her. She wished she'd asked the girl for her mobile number.

'Right,' said Fran, 'it's past nine o'clock. Let's go up and get our things, then we'll see what's happening with the workshop.'

***

Fran and Evie pushed open the door to the art room. There they found only Aggie, George and Helen, perched on tables, talking in low voices. No equipment had been set out, the yoghurt pots had not been filled and the projector not switched on.

'Hello,' said Aggie. 'I'm glad you're both here. We are just trying to decide what to do. Jean popped in to say she's leaving.

Her son is driving up to collect her today.'

'And we just saw Kayleigh,' said Fran. 'She's leaving too.'

'Oh,' said Aggie, visibly disappointed. 'So there's just the four of you. What are your feelings about the workshop. Should we continue? Is it a bit heartless to carry on?'

'I've got a train ticket booked for Saturday,' said George, bullish and blunt as usual. 'I paid for ten days and I'd like to get the ten days. I don't see why we should stop.'

Aggie looked at the sisters, questioningly. 'I'd like to stay,' said Evie. 'I want to find out what happened to the Americans. And if we don't paint, we'd just be moping about the hotel, fretting and looking at our phones all the time. Painting will stop us thinking morbid thoughts.'

'But it's up to you, Aggie,' said Fran. 'If you don't feel right carrying on, we'd understand.'

'What about you, Helen?' Aggie asked the quiet widow.

'I'd quite like to stay. I'm really rather enjoying the sessions, and, besides, my children are coming to fetch me at the weekend, too.'

'So, that's decided,' said Aggie. 'We'll carry on. I gave Roddy the day off today, so we don't have the minivan, but in any case, the forecast is poor this afternoon. So how about we work on skies today; dramatic stormy skies, blue skies, different methods of making clouds, working wet on wet and letting the paint bleed downwards, or wet on dry. Let's start by looking out of the window and just observing the different colours in the clouds today.'

Once again the morning seemed to pass in a heartbeat. Aggie got them to divide a big sheet of paper into eight squares and draw the same simple mountain outline on each. She demonstrated different effects on her own projected sheet: sunsets, storms, fluffy white clouds, angry dark clouds, cloudbursts etc, and the four amateurs tried to copy each one, the idea being to work quickly and spontaneously. Evie felt she'd learnt a lot. All thoughts of murder were banished as she concentrated on her paper.

After lunch the theme continued, and the group were encouraged to scale up the sky they liked best on a single sheet. Evie had mixed a moody combination of indigo and Payne's grey with a hint of purple on her pallet, and was just about to apply it onto the wet paper when she was aware of her mobile phone ringing. She ignored it and the ringing stopped, but then immediately started again. Reluctantly, she fetched it from her bag and glanced at the screen. Two missed calls. Jake. What the hell did he want? She was tempted to ignore the calls again, but when an SMS popped up saying 'call me asap!' she decided it must be important. She excused herself and made the call out in the corridor.

Jake answered immediately. 'Evie, thanks for calling back,' he said.

'Is everything OK?' she asked. 'Are your parents OK?'

'Yes, they're fine. Don't worry about that. But I got a phone call from your mum. She's worried sick about you and Fran. She made me promise to get you back home. So tell me what's been going on?'

Evie was surprised by his tone of voice. It was completely normal, as if they'd spoken for the last time only days ago, instead of months ago. It would be so easy to fall into the easy, chatty, jokey tone they used to share, but she was still on her guard. She must harden her heart. He had a new girlfriend after all, she didn't need to share things with him. Instead she kept things brief:

'Three murders, either connected to, or near the hotel. And I had a vision of the first murder.'

'OK,' he said slowly. 'You had a vision. Three murders. I think I'm with your mum. I think you should leave.'

'But you're not really in a position to tell me what to do, are you? We're not together any more.'

Jake sighed, exasperated. 'But I still care about you! I love you. I don't want anything to happen to you. And this sounds bloody dangerous.'

'I've got to stay, Jake, I've got to see it through. I feel I have to. I'm connected to this thing somehow.'

'Because you had a bloody vision?'

'Well, yes. I might be able to help catch whoever's doing this.'

'Fuck's sake! That's not your job! That's up to the police. You're putting yourself in danger.'

'Look, I'm never going to be on my own. I'm not going to do anything stupid. I'll be fine. We'll talk about it when I get back.'

'If you're not going to leave, maybe I'll come up to Scotland and get you.'

'God, Jake, don't treat me like a baby.' Evie let her annoyance show in her voice. 'I know what I'm doing. I'm not in any danger. Mum just went off on one of her usual doom scenarios, you know what she's like.'

'I don't like this...'

'You don't have to like it. It's really nothing to do with you..'

'Really? Really Evie? You're nothing to do with me? You're my wife, for God's sake.'

'Yes, I am...' She left a beat of silence, then added: 'For now.'

Jake's voice dropped to a hoarse whisper. 'So that's how you feel, is it? Well, in that case, I won't bother you any more. Goodbye Evie. You take care of yourself.'

'Bye,' said Evie, but he had already hung up.

Evie re-entered the art room with a frown. She felt confused. He'd been angry, he'd shouted, he'd sworn at her. But he'd also said he loved her. That he cared. What did that mean? Was it just residual loyalty, an acknowledgement of their shared years together? Evie knew without a shadow of doubt that she still loved Jake. She'd tried to let go, but it wasn't working. His voice had triggered a surge of longing to see him, to feel him close, to be with him. But did he love her? There she was much less sure.

'Who was that?' whispered Fran.

'Tell you later,' Evie whispered back.

At just before five o'clock, the group began to pack away their things and rinse their brushes. 'The forecast is good for tomorrow,' said Aggie. 'Would you like to go somewhere, or would you prefer to stay in the hotel? Don't decide now, we can talk about it in the morning. Good work today, people! Have a nice evening!'

Fran and Evie made their way down the corridor towards reception.

'You looked upset after that phone call,' said Fran. 'Who was it? The police? Is there news?'

'No. Mum got Jake to call me. I expect she thought a man would be more persuasive about getting us to leave. He was pretty angry that I wanted to stay.'

'He's probably just worried about you. I always liked him – you know that. You were so good together. Don't you think there's a chance...'

'I don't know. I just don't have a bloody clue any more.' Tears were falling down Evie's face and Fran gave her a hug.

'Sorry, I shouldn't have said anything. I'll keep my big mouth shut. So anyway, what do you want to do before dinner? Have a couple of drinks in the bar?'

'No. What I really want to do is go up to one of our rooms and get stuck into some research. Look into Arthur Ross. See if there's anything more about the French girl, or about Marge and Brett. Are you up for that? Will looking at a screen give you another headache? I don't mind doing it on my own.'

'No, that's fine. Two heads are better than one. Lead on, Nancy Drew!'

'Shall we buy a bottle to take up with us?'

'Go on then.'

Once seated on the big double bed in Fran's room, each with a glass of wine nearby, they started the search. Evie had pulled over the hotel's complimentary notepaper and pen and placed them beside her phone. Fran fired up the laptop she'd brought in case of work emergencies.

'Let's start with Arthur Ross,' she said.

There wasn't much to find. He appeared to be the author of three books on Scottish history, which were serious and critically acclaimed. But the author biography was scant. He had studied history and anthropology at Oxford and lived in St Albans. There was nothing about his birthplace, family status or personal history. There was a photo of him on the inside cover of one of the books that Evie was able to look inside on Amazon, in which he appeared unsmiling, dressed in black against a plain white background. They learnt nothing from the photo.

'OK, let's try the French influencer girl. Can you remember her name?' asked Evie.

'Yes, Escoffier. I can't remember her first name.'

'How the hell did you remember that?'

'I remember thinking it's the same as the detective in that French series, Spiral. Did you ever watch it?'

'No. But that's great. I'm putting 'Escoffier Skye influencer murder' into Google,' she said as her thumb flew over the phone's screen.

'I'll try French Instagrammer death Skye' said Fran, typing on the laptop.

Evie clicked on a link and started reading. 'That's not right', she said, puzzled, and clicked on another. Then another. 'This can't be right!' she said again. 'Have you got a photo?' she asked Fran.

'Yes, look.' Fran turned the laptop round so Evie could see.

'It's not the same girl,' Evie said.

'What d'you mean?' asked Fran.

'My vision was very clear. It was a girl with long blonde hair, very pale skin, pale eyes. This girl looks like she might be of North African descent, Moroccan maybe, or mixed race. Look at her hair - it's dark, and those corkscrew curls. Brown eyes. And her skin is really matt.'

'That's weird. Did she change her hair colour perhaps? Get contact lenses?'

'I don't know. It's possible, I suppose. But I think it might be a different girl. Let me think. What does this mean... Let's read the articles.'

A few minutes later, Evie said 'Shit!' All colour had gone from her cheeks, and she looked scared.

'What is it?'

'It's obvious, Fran. Think. In all the time you've known me, and known about the flashes, have I ever had a vision that showed a past event?'

'Um... I can't think of one.'

'No, I never get flashbacks, they're always premonitions, it's always about the future. So either this is another murder that happened after we arrived here, and no-one has found her yet, or else it's a murder that hasn't taken place yet.'

'Oh my God! Are you sure?'

'I'm sure.'

'Holy shit. Shall we phone the police?' asked Fran.

'They won't take it seriously. Can you imagine? 'The girl in my vision had blonde hair, not dark, her skin was pale'... They're not going to do anything! That snide, younger detective pretty much laughed at the idea of visions.'

'Look,' said Fran, conscious that Evie's voice was edging on panic. 'Let's have a break. Let's go and get some fresh air in the gardens, then take a shower and go down for dinner, think about something else for a while. Then we'll figure out what to do with a clear head.'

'OK. Good idea, I need a break.'

It was cold outside but the sharp wind blew colour into their cheeks as they walked round the walled gardens. Evie felt her head begin to clear as she gazed at the tall trees beyond the wall and the pair of buzzards circling above them, heads twitching side to side as they searched for prey. Their calls sounded eerily like children crying. Back in their rooms, they showered, dressed and came down once more to eat dinner in the half-empty dining room. There was no sign of Arthur Ross. Helen and George were sitting together at a table nearby; and the four hill walkers had spread their map out on their table, and were leaning over it, plotting the next day's route. Evie and Fran ate their Arbroath smokies in thoughtful silence, then adjourned to the bar for their coffee.

'Ladies, what can I get you?' They were surprised to see Roddy behind the bar, wiping glasses and polishing the counter. He wore his usual fisherman's sweater. His reddish-brown hair was unkempt and fell into his eyes, but his smile was warm.

'Ah, so you're mountain guide, fishing guide, chauffeur and also barman, are you?' said Evie, teasingly.

'Just filling in while wee Jamie's away having his dinner,' said Roddy. 'So what'll it be?'

'Just two coffees please,' said Fran. 'Milky ones.'

'Take a seat and I'll bring them over,' said Roddy.

The bar was empty, apart from the German couple. Fran and Evie sat back in the comfortable velvet armchairs and both sighed as they felt their spines unwind. It had been a long day.

Roddy brought the coffees to their table, and also two small glasses filled with amber liquid.

'I thought you might like to try the local whisky, too. It's Talisker. My treat. You both look fair peely-wally, if you don't mind me saying?'

'Well, that depends what peely-wally means,' said Fran.

'Och, it's just you both look a bit pale. And it's no wonder, with what's been going on around here. But I'm glad you both decided to stay. The weather's looking up and tomorrow's going to be a cracker.' With that, he left them and returned to the bar.

Fran took a sip of the whisky. 'Mm, it's good!' she said. 'Listen, I've got an idea. Can you remember the place in your vision? A tumbledown churchyard, wasn't it?'

'Yes, I remember it clearly.'

'Could you try and draw it?'

'Yes, I think so.'

'I'll ask the girl at reception if they've got paper and a pencil.'

Fran returned with a notepad and a nice sharp pencil. Evie closed her eyes, concentrated for a few moments, then began to sketch. She started with the crumbling apex wall with its pointed peak and narrow bricked-up slit of a window. She added the long, wispy grasses and lush ivy growing up between the stone blocks. She then outlined the twisted yew tree behind it, and finally the gravestones, which slanted this way and that on the grassy mound below. One gravestone was topped with a fine, intricately carved Celtic cross. When she was satisfied she showed it to Fran.

'Wow, that's detailed,' said Fran. She looked over at the bar, where Roddy was chatting with the barman, Jamie. She had an idea. 'What if we showed it to Roddy? He seems to know every inch of the island. Then at least we'd know what place this is.'

Evie hesitated, reluctant to bring someone else into the discussion. 'Well, I suppose we could. Do we trust him?'

'I think we can trust him. He's never been anything but kind and helpful to us. Should we? We could do with an ally.'

'Yeah, OK then.'

Fran walked over to the bar. 'Can I buy you back a drink,

Roddy? And we've got a favour to ask, if you're not busy.'

Roddy looked surprised, but pleased. 'Aye, sure. I'll have a pint of Tennents, thanks.'

Back at the table, Roddy sat down and took a long pull at his beer. He was wearing his faded kilt, as usual. Both feet were planted on the floor and his knees were splayed. Curly twists of reddish hair were visible over his thick walking socks. He's very comfortable in his own body, thought Evie. Totally at ease. He's like Jake in that way. Again she felt the tug of attraction to this solid Highlander. She forced herself to look away.

'Right, ladies, what can I do for you?' he asked, looking expectantly from one to the other.

Wordlessly, Evie opened the notebook at the page with the sketch and pushed it across the table to Roddy.

'Wow,' he said, 'that's really good! Is that what you were sketching just now?'

'Yeah.'

'It's really realistic. Did you use a photo on your phone?'

'Um, no, it's um, from memory.'

'You must have a photographic memory, then. It's dead accurate. I didn't know you'd visited the old church.'

'So you know where it is?'

'Yes, of course.' Roddy looked at Evie strangely. 'Like I said, it's instantly recognisable.'

'So where is it?' asked Fran.

Roddy now looked totally confused. 'It's Cill Criosd, the ruined church. We drove past it a couple of days ago on the way to Elgol.'

'Thanks, Roddy,' said Fran. She and Evie stared at each other, mutely, wondering what to do next. A long moment passed.

'Look, tell me if it's none of my business, but you both look like you're worried sick. Are you in some kind of trouble? Is it anything to do with these murders?' Despite the tension of the moment, Evie was captivated by the way he rolled his Rs over the word 'murder'.

Fran looked questioningly at Evie, and Evie knew she was silently asking 'should we tell him?' Still Evie hesitated. They needed an ally but was Roddy the right person? Would he believe them? Eventually she gave a slight nod.

'We think there's been another murder,' said Fran. 'Or else there's about to be one.'

Roddy remained silent, waiting for them to expand.

'I had a premonition,' continued Evie. 'Of a dead blonde girl lying on a gravestone at this place.'

Roddy frowned into his beer. 'You don't think it was just a bad dream?' he asked.

'I've always had premonitions. Since I was a kid. They pretty well always come true.'

'OK,' he said, slowly. He seemed to be taking things seriously, and Evie was relieved. 'In that case you must call the police right now and tell them to go and look at the church.'

'But I'm scared I'll send them off on a wild goose chase, and they'll think I'm wasting their time. One of the detectives was really sceptical when I told him about the vision. He more or less said it was a load of crap.'

'Well, what do you want to do? How can I help?'

'I don't know.'

Roddy paused, his expression thoughtful. 'Well, if you want, I could drive you both to the church tomorrow morning, first thing. We'd be back in time for the workshop, it's not too far. And if there's nothing, at least your minds will be at rest. If there's something, well, then we contact the police.'

'Would you do that for us?'

'Of course I would. Nae bother. What do you say?'

The sisters looked at each other, their eyebrows raised

questioningly. Without needing to speak, a decision was made.

'OK.'

'Shall we meet in the reception at about seven tomorrow morning?'

'Roddy, that's really good of you. Thanks so much!'

'Nae bother at all. I'm more than happy to help. Now, another drink?'

'No thanks, we'd better get to bed if we're up early,' said Fran. 'Thanks again. See you tomorrow.'

As they rose from their seats, Roddy rose also with a light bow. 'Have a good night, and try not to worry,' he said. 'Everything's going to be OK.'

C HAPTER TWELVE: CILL CRIOSD

Evie woke at six when her phone alarm went off. She'd slept well and felt alert and almost excited. At last they were taking some action, instead of sitting around speculating and worrying. She dressed quickly and went to knock on Fran's door.

One look at Fran's face told her the worst. Fran was still in her pyjamas. Her short brown hair was sticking up in damp spikes. One eye was covered by her hand, and the other eye was dark pink, the eyelid swollen.

'Migraine?'

'Yep, awful one. I'm not going to be able to go this morning.'

'No, of course not. I'll stay here with you,' said Evie. 'You need me here.' She tried to hide her disappointment, but Fran could see right through her.

'You really want to go, don't you?' asked Fran.

'I feel almost compelled to go, yes.'

'But we promised we'd stick together. It might not be safe.'

'I think I'll be safe enough with Roddy. He's strong enough to fight off any attackers.'

'Will you be safe with him though?'

'What do you mean, you don't think he's the killer, do you?'

'No, course not, but he might make a move on you. He obviously likes you.'

'Don't worry about that, I'll be fine.'

'Listen, can you fetch my handbag over there?'

Evie fetched the voluminous leather bag from the chair

where it was sitting.

'Here, take this. Pepper spray,' said Fran, holding out a small black and red cannister.

'What are you doing with pepper spray? It's illegal isn't it?'

'Yes, technically. But I work late so often and have to walk to the tube in the dark. I feel safer with it, especially since the Sarah Everard case,' said Fran, thinking back to the abduction and murder of the beautiful young woman in South London a few years previously.

'OK, I'll take it with me. It's small isn't it? Fits in a pocket OK.'

'Yep, practical.'

'So is this for if Roddy jumps on me, or for the killer?' said Evie, attempting a feeble joke.

'Works well in both cases,' said Fran with an equally weak smile.

'Is there anything I can get you before I go? Have you got water, pills?'

'I'm fine. Now go!' said Fran, pushing Evie towards the door. 'And be careful!'

Evie slipped the spray in her jacket pocket and walked down the stairs. Roddy was waiting at reception. He was wearing jeans today, with his fisherman's sweater and an old waxed jacket, and Evie was glad not to have the distraction of his hairy knees.

'Fran's not coming,' said Evie. 'She's got a really bad migraine.'

'Oh!' Roddy looked concerned. 'Well, listen, do you want to cancel the trip? You might not want to go with just me. We can do it another time when your sister's feeling better?'

'No, if it's OK, I want to go now. I feel it could be important.'

'OK then, let's go. My car's round the back of the stables.'

He led the way around the side of the hotel to the stable

block, where a battered black Ford Fiesta stood.

'The car's a midden, I'm afraid. And it smells a bit of fish,' said Roddy apologetically.

'Oh, don't worry about that. As long as it goes,' said Evie, brushing a few sweet wrappers onto the footwell and getting into the passenger seat. There was in fact quite a fishy smell.

Roddy kept up a stream of light chat as they drove south. He seemed aware that Evie was keyed up, and so steered her thoughts away from their task by asking questions about her job at Leeds Council, her flat, and her parents. In turn he told Evie about his family, most of whom had left Skye to go and live on the mainland.

'But why did they leave?' asked Evie. 'It's so beautiful here.'

'Mam and Dad wanted to be nearer a city with a decent hospital for when they retire – and they wanted to move now so they could start making friends. They're in Dundee. And my brother Calum left for his studies in Glasgow and never came back.'

'But you never felt like leaving?'

'Never. You'll have to carry me off this island in a box!' he said cheerfully. 'I could never leave this place.'

He laughed and Evie was again struck by his light-hearted manner. Why is he so upbeat, she wondered? He can't really believe we're looking for a body. Is he just humouring me? Or maybe he's just being kind. He's trying to downplay this crazy goose chase that we're on, to make it seem normal. He knows how nervous I am.

The journey passed very quickly, and soon they were off the main road and once more travelling along the rough, single-track road, and dodging the sleepy sheep with their ragged coats.

'Why don't they shear the sheep here?' asked Evie.

'I'm not sure. They should shear them; it's much better for the sheep. The wool gets really heavy and waterlogged if not. But

I guess the farmer here has a problem of some sort.'

This information only added to the feeling of isolation, of neglect, in the valley. It was incredibly beautiful, with the Red Cuillins glowing a rusty brown in the sunshine, but the desolation still made Evie shiver.

'There it is,' said Roddy, as the ruined church came into view on the right. He slowed the car to a crawl and glanced over at Evie. There was something a little unsettling in his regard; a strange gleam in his eyes. Is he excited about this, wondered Evie? Does he think it's an adventure, a game? She herself was dreading it.

'What do you want to do?' he asked. 'Shall I go and look first?'

'No, it's OK. I'll come.'

Roddy stopped the car at the side of the road and looked at Evie expectantly, waiting for her to take the lead. Evie looked up at the roofless church, which stood forlornly on the crest of the hill. She felt suddenly sick with apprehension.

'OK,' she said, slowly, mustering her courage. 'In my vision the yew tree was behind the back wall, that one with the bricked up window. So I guess if there's a body, it will be at the foot of the hill, on the right.'

They got out of the car and went through a gate in the low stone wall.

'Ready?' asked Roddy.

'Ready,' said Evie. Roddy took her hand, and together they walked through the short grass. Two sheep stopped munching and stared at them with disinterest as they picked their way past the gravestones.

Evie stopped abruptly. 'There's something there!' she said. A pale shape was partly visible through the longer grasses a little further up.

'Do you want me to..?' asked Roddy again.

'No, come on.' Evie set her jaw and took a deep steadying breath.

They walked slowly further until the object came into clearer view.

'Oh God! Oh God,' breathed Evie. It was just as her vision had shown her; the pale alabaster limbs posed with precision, the arms crossed over the chest, the bright red toenail varnish, the blonde hair fanning out behind the head… But the head!

'No!' wailed Evie, 'Oh please God, no!'

'Is that…? said Roddy.

'It's Kayleigh! Oh my God, no, no!' She made to run the last few steps to the body, but Roddy grabbed her arm to hold her back.

'Wait! You mustn't go too near. It's a crime scene.'

Tears poured down Evie's face and she dashed them away with one hand. 'But we can't just leave her like that! It's Kayleigh! Is she… are you sure she's dead?' Evie knew from the sightless, pale blue eyes, staring up into the sky, that there was no hope, but her mind would not accept it.

'There's no doubt,' said Roddy. 'I'm so sorry.'

'Can we at least cover her up with something?'

'We mustn't change anything. It's hard, but we can't touch anything. We've got to phone the police.' He took his mobile out of his jeans pocket and looked at the screen. 'The signal's really bad here. I've got no bars. What about you?'

Evie took her own phone out of her pocket. 'No, no bars either. Shit, shit!'

'Let's have a wee think. If we drive back towards Broadford we should get a signal.'

'I don't want to leave her. The sheep, those crows. They might… It's too awful.'

'We must. We've got to go. Come on.'

Roddy tugged her arm and reluctantly Evie tore her gaze

away from the macabre sight and followed him down the hill and back through the gate. Just as they reached the car, she suddenly bent double, put a hand on the low wall and retched violently into the grass, over and over again. Roddy put his left arm round her shoulders, and with his right hand he held back her hair, until, finally, the vomiting stopped.

'You're shivering like crazy,' he said, when she was able to stand straight again. 'You're in shock. I've got a blanket in the boot.' He opened the boot and rummaged amongst the messy objects there: a box of fishing bait, walking poles, an ancient anorak, until he found an old tartan blanket and wrapped it round her shoulders.

'Sorry, it's really fishy,' he said.

Evie nodded her thanks. She could not speak. She could not look at him. She needed a moment to think. As Roddy had pushed aside the various items to get to the blanket, she had caught sight of something. A bulging black bin bag, not completely shut but tied loosely at the top. And peaking out between the gathered yellow drawstrings was something white. White leather. White leather, like Kayleigh's fashion boots. Wordlessly, she got into the car and Roddy started the engine.

'OK? Feeling better?' he asked, and again she nodded, without looking over. She shut her eyes and tried to think. What objects are made of white leather? What else could it be? Fishing equipment? Walking gloves? Binocular case? Unlikely, she thought. But trainers… Everyone has white trainers. Maybe Roddy keeps his trainers in the boot of the car. She tried to remember if Roddy had been dancing in his walking boots at the ceilidh. She thought not. He could have been wearing trainers. But white? She couldn't quite picture it. But it couldn't be Roddy, it just couldn't. He's gentle, thoughtful, decent. She risked a quick glance across at him. He looked just the same; calm and caring, concentrating on the road ahead, his strong hands light on the steering wheel. She was still see-sawing madly between doubt and certainty when Roddy stopped the car.

'Why are we stopping here?' she asked.

'There's a phone mast just over that hill,' said Roddy, dipping his head and pointing through the side window to a low hill topped with a slew of craggy rocks and boulders. 'We'll get a signal up there for sure.'

'Shouldn't be continue to Portree? Go straight to the police station direct?'

'Yes, for sure we could, if you feel more comfortable doing that? It's completely up to you.' He paused and looked at her, and Evie tried to read his expression. It was open, questioning, concerned. There was no hint of stress or impatience or tension. 'But I thought it'd be better if we phone the police as quick as possible,' he continued, 'then we can double back and meet them at the church when they come. It'll save both us and the police a lot of time.'

Evie saw the logic in this, but still she hesitated. Was he...? Could he be...? No, it's impossible. No way. She made up her mind. 'OK,' she said at last, and put her hand on the car door handle. Roddy smiled at her, encouragingly, then opened his own door. Evie noted that he left the key in the ignition. She checked the bulge in her pocket and felt the reassuring shape of the pepper spray.

They started to climb up a narrow sheep track through the heather. The hill was low, but steep, and Roddy grabbed her hand to pull her up the difficult stretches of loose rocks. Glancing up, Evie noticed that the weather was changing slightly. Tendrils of mist were snaking down from the higher mountains, reaching probing fingers towards them. She shivered. When they eventually made it to the top, Roddy gestured to the boulders.

'Sit down, get your breath back,' he said, 'and let's check our phones.'

Evie pulled her phone out once again and checked the signal. Dismayed, she saw that there were still no bars. She looked up at Roddy, expecting him to be doing the same, but he didn't have his phone in his hand. He was looking at her, kindly, almost pityingly. A horrible, cold feeling of dread started to creep into her soul. She must keep calm, she mustn't show him that she had doubts.

'Nothing. Still nothing. Let's drive to Broadford and try there,' she said.

But instead, Roddy sat down on a rock, facing her. He still had that gentle, pitying smile on his face.

'No, I think we need to talk. You saw the boots didn't you?'

'What boots?'

'You saw Kayleigh's white boots.'

'I don't know what you're talking about!' Oh fuck, oh fuck, Evie thought.

'Come now, Evie. Your face gives away everything you're feeling, you can't hide it. I know you saw Kayleigh's boots in my car.'

Evie said nothing. She stared across at him, her mind racing. Deny it? But he'd just admitted they were Kayleigh's boots. There was no point pretending any more.

'Did you kill Kayleigh?' she asked at last in a small, flat voice.

Roddy nodded. 'Yes, I did. But I think you'll understand. I know you'll understand. You're like me; you get how magical this island is. You understand that we need to protect it.'

'I don't, I don't understand. What's that got to do with Kayleigh?' Another thought raced into her head. 'Did you kill the French girl? And the Americans?'

'I did. But I'll explain. I know you'll understand.' He paused and Evie looked around, hoping against hope to see a car, or a farmhouse, or a hiker. But there was nothing. Silence. Just a slight breeze that blew her hair into her eyes and the wailing cry of a buzzard overhead. The mist was thickening, creeping insidiously towards them and gradually shrouding the mountain above. She was quite alone with a killer.

Roddy began to talk. His voice was calm and patient and musical; he could have been reading a bedtime story to a child.

'It started when I was walking the Skye trail with two brothers from Manchester. They'd hired me as a guide. It's a difficult trail; it's not marked and it's dangerous in places. We'd decided to do it in reverse. We started at Broadford, then went down to Elgol and then headed up north towards Portree. It can take about seven days, if you don't meet any problems, and it's challenging. We had our tents on our backs and the weather was mixed. But the scenery is so, so beautiful. And if you walk it, you really get to experience everything - the calls of birds, the smell of the heather, the taste of the rain - you can really appreciate it. We'd just done a very tough stretch, the Trottenish Ridge, and the Old Man of Storr – those incredible needle peaks. And we were approaching the Quiraing, which is another just magical place, stunning. And you know, we felt we really deserved it, we'd earned our right to be there.

'Just as we got there, and began to take in the views, a car sped up the road, driving way too fast. A bright green VW Beetle. It parked on the road, half blocking it. A woman got out. Thin. Long brown hair. She walked ten metres. She got out her phone, and messed with her hair. Then she pouted and took a selfie, then another from above, then another. She never even looked round at the view. She looked at her phone, then attached one of those selfie-stick things and took a few more. Then got back in her car, wound the window down, ate a bar of something and threw the wrapper out of the window. Wound the window back up, turned round and drove off again, far too fast, making the motor roar and breaking the silence. And I hated her. I hated her with every fibre of my being. She was everything that's wrong with tourists in this place. Didn't give a fuck about the island, the mountains, the heather - just wanted it as a backdrop to her own self-glorifying story. I picked up the wrapper and said something to the two brothers, and we laughed. But I was sick, pure sick with hatred.

'A few days later, we'd finished the trail and I was in Portree. I saw this woman's car in the car park. There was no mistaking it. Bright green. So when she came back to it I followed her in my car. She drove off to her Airbnb – one of those super-modern metal boxes with huge windows in Carbost – quite near the hotel, but still really remote. And I knocked on the door. I just wanted to give her back her bloody wrapper, or stick it down her throat or...challenge her in some way, give her a bollocking, or... I don't know what. But when she opened the door, and I saw her, she gave this sexy smile and looked me up and down and said something suggestive in her strong French accent and... I just lost it. I strangled her. I put my hands round her throat until she went limp. Then I sat outside her Airbnb for ages thinking about what to do. I couldn't believe what I'd done. Should I call the police, admit it, or say I found her that way, or hide the body? Then it came to me. Such a simple idea.' He smiled happily. 'I had killed a tourist. It was done. I would make it work for the good of the island. I would stage the body so it had maximum impact, so it looked like some kind of Druid ceremony, and got reported in the papers.'

'But why? I don't get it.'

'It's obvious, Evie! Think! Tourists are ruining the island. Too many, the wrong kind. The demonstrations aren't putting anyone off. Slashing tyres, painting graffiti – it's all such small fry. So we need something more... more persuasive, more drastic. You wouldn't go on holiday to, say Minorca, if there'd been a horrible murder there, would you?'

'I don't know, I might. People never think it'll happen to them.'

Roddy shrugged. His eyes had taken on a slightly mad gleam. 'So that was the start. I had killed an influencer. Then I started thinking of all the other tourists who ruin this place. The ones who come in their hoards. Americans. Those loud, insensitive fourth generation Americans who still think they're

Scottish because their great, great grandfather came from the islands and their surname sounds a wee bit Scottish. The ones who buy their clan tartan because their name is Blair, or something, and have the bloody nerve to think they can wear it.'

'So you killed Marge and Brett.' It was not a question.

'I did. I followed them in my car as they visited various sites. When they parked up by the broch and began to walk up the hill, I knew I could get them. It's quiet up there, you see, well off the beaten track. Nobody around. So I walked up behind them. Picked up a nice heavy stone and hit them both over the head. Then I lay them side by side and crossed their arms, like the girl's, so it looked a bit occultist. I walked down, moved their car, walked back for my car. It was easy, really easy.'

'But what about Kayleigh? What had she ever done? She wasn't one of the bad tourists, she was trying to appreciate the place, trying to paint it.'

'Aye, she wasn't a bad wee lassie. I liked her a lot. But that day when we were skimming stones in Uignish, she told me who her father is. He is really famous! That was just too good an opportunity to miss. Can you imagine the headlines in the papers tomorrow? It'll be front page all over the UK. 'TV chef's daughter killed in bizarre satanic ritual.' 'Skye murder mystery of TV chef's daughter.'' Roddy's hand drew lines in the air as he imagined the headlines. His eyes were shining. 'They'll link it to the other murders, and there'll be a panic about serial killers. Tourist numbers will plummet, I'm telling you! People will be cancelling their hotels, their campsites, their Airbnbs, their ferries. It's going to start happening tomorrow, I promise you!'

'How did you kill her?'

'Again, it was almost too easy. The opportunity just fell into my lap. I offered her a lift to Kyle to save the taxi fare. I asked her not to tell anyone, 'cos I was supposed to be available for Aggie and you art ladies, so we sneaked off on the quiet. We stopped on a quiet bit of road and I pulled her towards me for a wee kiss –

she was more than willing, and I did kiss her. So, you see, her last moments were pleasant.' Roddy smiled, and Evie was revulsed. He actually thought he'd been good to the poor girl. 'Then I strangled her. Brought her to the church. You can guess the rest.'

Evie took a few moments before she was able to speak. Then she asked: 'So is that the end of it? Have you finished?'

'No, I'm not done yet. I'm going to target the cruise ship passengers next.'

'How are you going to do that? They all stick together in big groups!' Despite herself and in spite of the horror of his words, Evie was intrigued.

'I've got a plan. I know exactly what I'm going to do. So what do you think, Evie? Can you see the beauty of it?' He looked at her, earnestly. 'You appreciate this island, I know you do. You see how it needs protecting. You can see what I'm trying to do, can't you?'

Christ, thought Evie, he really thinks I'm going to agree with him! Congratulate him even! But there's a chance he'll let me go if he thinks I'm on his side. I must be careful. 'Well,' she said, slowly, 'I can fully understand your objectives. But your methods... They're drastic! Isn't there another way? A kinder way?'

'I know what you mean. It took me a while to get my head round it, too. It's brutal, but it's a necessary sacrifice. For the loss of a few lives the island will be transformed. Airbnbs will go out of business and be changed back into houses that locals can afford. There'll be no more rubbish dumped on the roadsides, no more erosion of the footpaths, no more building huge ugly car parks. No more massive tour buses queuing up at the beauty spots and disgorging hundreds at a time. The locals will be able to visit their favourite places once again. It'll be quiet, peaceful, like it was a hundred years ago. The spirituality of this place, it's being lost at the moment. The majesty. These day-trippers, they treat Skye like a theme park experience. Jump on, take a photo, jump off. Where's their sense of awe, of wonder?'

'But it won't last. People forget so quickly. After a couple of years they'll come back in even bigger numbers, won't they?'

'Then I'll have to do another one.' Again that happy smile. 'Maybe one murder every year.'

Oh God, he's mad, totally mad, thought Evie, but she kept her face open and interested. 'What about the people who depend on tourism? The hotels, the tourist boats, the restaurants?' she asked.

'Well, that's the beauty of it. We'll attract a better, more thoughtful kind of tourist. One who actually spends a few days here, spends some money, hires an e-bike or hires a guide. Goes fishing, goes hiking, paints! It won't be just a place people cross off their bucket list, like stupid wee sheep following the herd, it'll be a place of mystery, an almost spiritual experience, for people with a brain, people who want to discover and learn. And those people act respectfully. They actually spend money – they go to the restaurants, they buy things in craft shops, they take trips to the other islands, so the economy will benefit.'

'I'm beginning to see what you mean. I'm just... I'm just sad about Kayleigh. I really liked her.' Evie hoped she sounded convincing. Her skin was crawling with disgust and her heart was thumping in her chest, but she fought to keep her voice calm.

'I knew you'd get it!' Roddy beamed at her, delighted. 'You won't turn me in, will you? You see how necessary all this is. You're one of the good ones.' He stood up, took a step towards her, then pulled Evie to her feet. Still smiling happily, he placed both hands on the collar of her jacket and bent his head towards her. She realised, with revulsion, that he was about to kiss her. She jerked her head back violently then twisted it away to the side, screwing up her eyes.

'Och, no,' said Roddy. His voice was once again soft and pitying. 'So that's the way the land lies, is it, ma wee lassie?' He put a hand on her chin and forced her head round to face him. 'You've been stringing me along, haven't you?'

Evie stared into his golden eyes. His expression was full of compassion and sadness. 'No, no, it's just… I'm married. I don't like you in that way, but I understand…'

He cut her off mid-sentence. 'I can see right through you. You're so transparent. You're scared of me. You think I'm crazy, don't you? God, this is a shame. I liked you, I really did. I don't want to kill you but I have no choice now. I'll make it really quick. That's the best I can do for you.'

One hand crept from chin to throat, the other hand joined it, and he began to apply pressure. Evie could feel his thumbs pushing into her neck. She had to act fast before she lost consciousness. She scrabbled blindly for her jacket pocket, unzipped it and felt the reassuring coolness of the pepper spray. God, I didn't even look how you use it, she panicked. How stupid! Is there a cap? Which side does the spray come out? Quick, quick! Her vision was starting to blur. She felt nauseous and light-headed. With one gigantic last effort she lifted the canister, aimed it into those golden eyes and pressed her thumb down hard. A stream of liquid shot out directly into Roddy's face, blinding him. He yelled, let go of her and rubbed at his eyes, staggering backwards. Evie did not hesitate. She aimed a foot at his groin and kicked him as hard as she possibly could. Roddy doubled over in pain and Evie aimed another kick at his head. Roddy's hand shot out, trying to catch her foot, but he could no longer see and Evie skipped away. Then she ran, as fast as her trembling legs would allow, back down the hill, slipping and skidding on the loose stones, catching her feet in the heather, almost falling, but keeping upright, until she made it to the car. She yanked open the door, threw herself into the drivers seat and turned the key. Oh, thank God, thank God, she prayed, as the engine started first time.

CHAPTER THIRTEEN: PORTREE

Evie had no idea how she managed to drive the next few miles. Her feet only just reached the pedals as she perched on the edge of the seat. Her hands were trembling on the steering wheel, her foot jerky on the accelerator. Her only thought was to get away, as fast as she could. She narrowly avoided a sheep as she careered over a blind summit. When she reached the outskirts of Broadford, and the first few reassuring houses came into sight, she slowed down to a stop and breathed in and out, in and out, slowly, until her heart stopped its hammering. She considered what to do next. She could phone the police now, but instinct told her to press on, to reach safety fast. She decided to drive to the main town, Portree, and find the police station. She adjusted the seat and the wing mirrors, clipped on the seatbelt, and drove at a more sedate pace along the main road north, putting as much distance as possible between herself and Roddy.

About forty minutes later, Evie reached Portree. It was no more than a village, with attractive multi-coloured cottages clustered around the harbour and dozens of little boats dotted about in the sheltered horseshoe bay, but Evie had no time to admire the views. She found the police station fairly easily, on the main square of the town, and her heart sank. The building was tiny, about the size of an average family house, with a discreet blue sign over the entrance and parking for barely half a dozen cars. The police here would be more used to directing traffic, breaking up bar brawls and investigating missing sheep than catching a murderer, she thought. She parked Roddy's car right by the entrance and ran through the door. The front desk was manned by a middle-aged woman with a curly perm and a gentle smile.

'Can I help you, dearie?' said the woman.

Evie was suddenly exhausted, and close to tears. The kindly expression on the woman's face was too much, and she started to sob.

'There, there, don't you worry, dearie; whatever it is, we'll sort it out. Here, have a tissue. Can I get you a glass of water or a cup of tea?'

'No, no,' said Evie, regaining some composure. 'I need to speak to Sergeant Reid and DS Sterling. It's urgent. It's about the murders.'

The woman's face changed instantly, and she became alert and efficient. 'And what's your name?' she asked.

'It's Evie Carpenter.'

'One second please. Take a seat over there.' She pointed to a row of hard plastic chairs.

A few minutes later, footsteps sounded in the corridor, the door opened, and DS Sterling appeared. Evie's heart dropped; she'd been desperately hoping to speak to Sergeant Reid, the older, more empathetic detective.

'Mrs Carpenter, what can I do for you?'

'There's been another murder,' she blurted out. 'And the killer is Roddy from the hotel.'

The detective's face did not change. 'I take it you've had another of your 'visions' then?' he said with ill-disguised derision.

'No,' said Evie, desperately trying to remain patient, 'I was with him an hour ago. He confessed. And he tried to strangle me.'

'I see. Yesterday you were convinced that Arthur Ross was the killer, and now you're telling me it's Roddy McAllister?'

'Yes, yes, Roddy from the hotel. And there's a body. It's at Cill Croisd, the old church on the road to Elgol. And it's Kayleigh

Petersen.'

DS Sterling sighed. 'You'd better come inside and make a statement, then,' he said, with reluctance. 'Follow me.' He led the way along the corridor and into a large open-plan room. Three policemen were sitting at desks, working on computers, and glanced up briefly as she entered. 'Have a seat,' said DS Sterling, pointing to an empty chair. He himself perched on the edge of his desk, obviously not planning to remain there for very long.

'So start at the beginning.'

'Well, I realised that the vision I had of the murder was not the French girl; the hair was wrong, and the toenails. So I thought I must have had a premonition of a different murder, or one that maybe hadn't happened yet. I drew a picture of the place I'd seen in my head, and Roddy said it was Cill Croisd church. He offered to drive me there this morning to check if there was a body. And we found Kayleigh there, lying on a grave marker, just like my vision. Roddy said we should call the police, and he said the signal was better up on a hill. So we walked up, and that's when he told me. He'd killed Kayleigh, the French girl and the American couple. He's mad, he's mad. And then he tried to kill me, but I got away and drove his car here. Oh, and his car is outside. I'm pretty sure there's evidence in it. Kayleigh's clothes are in a bin bag in the boot.' Evie paused, looking up at the impassive detective. 'Why aren't you taking notes? Why aren't you doing anything? His car is outside!'

He regarded her, head slightly on one side. 'I'm trying to work out what your game is. You enjoy being at the heart of things don't you, you get a thrill from the attention, I think.'

'God, you don't believe me! For Christ's sake, I'm not making this up!'

'I'm not sure if you're being deliberately obstructive, or if you've got a mental disorder of some kind that makes you invent stories to compensate for your...'

He was interrupted in mid-sentence. The door opened and

Sergeant Reid stood in the doorway.

'Jim,' he said, glancing quickly at Evie, then back to the detective. 'Come outside. We've got another one.'

'Another …?'

'Yes. Two tourists just called it in.'

'Where?'

'Not in front of Mrs Carpenter…'

Evie broke in. 'It's at Cill Croisd, isn't it? I was there. I saw it. I've been trying to tell your colleague…'

'What? You were there? Good God!' He took three quick paces into the room to stand in front of Evie. 'Tell us everything!'

And so Evie recounted her story again, in more detail this time, trying to leave nothing out. There followed a rush of activity. All the officers were called into the room, given a quick update on the new suspect, and then given hasty instructions by Sergeant Reid:

'George, drive to Cill Croisd now and preserve the scene, until we get there. Mary,' this to the older woman who had manned the front desk, 'Get in touch with the Inverness forensics team, see if they're still on the island. If they are, then get them to Cill Croisd asap. Dougie, I want you to go to the Old Manse Hotel and search the room Roddy McAllister's been using. Then see if you can find the art teacher, Aggie something, and see if she knows where he could be hiding.' Sergeant Reid paused, thinking hard.

'Oh, and Mary,' he continued, 'we need to find the home address of Roderick McAllister. Search the directory. Sandy, there's a car out front.' Here, Sergeant Reid turned and said to Evie: 'Have you got the keys?'

'Yes, here.' Evie handed them over. 'It's a black Ford Fiesta.'

'Right, thanks. Sandy, bring the car into the yard and search the boot. Bag up everything.'

DS Sterling now took over. 'I'll put out an all cars alert for

Roderick McAllister, for the north of Scotland,' he said. 'Mary, can you try and find a picture we can use?'

Evie sat back in her chair, totally spent, glad that things were now out of her hands. She started to shake.

'Are you OK?' asked Sergeant Reid. 'We should get you checked out by a doctor. Are you having difficulty breathing?'

'No, no, I'll be fine,' said Evie. 'But I really need to speak to my sister, if that's OK.'

'Of course! She should be here with you. Sandy, when you've brought the car in, can you drive to the Old Manse and find Francesca Lloyd. Tell her that her sister is at the police station and she's OK, but that she should come and be with her. Bring her here as quick as you can. You can bag up the evidence when you get back.' He looked at Evie kindly. 'You've had a big shock. We'd like you to stay here until we get back. We'll need to take a more detailed statement from you, one that we'll record. PC Carswell here will look after you until we get back.' The curly haired desk sergeant nodded and smiled reassuringly. 'She'll get you something to eat and show you where you can wait. Your sister will be here before you know it. Is that OK?'

'Yes, yes, fine.'

'Is there anything else we need to know before we go?'

'I don't think so.'

'Ok then. Let's get to it, everyone!'

Uniform jackets and hats were hastily grabbed from chairs and desks, and all hurried out of the room, which was then locked. Mary Carswell gestured for Evie to follow her.

'Come into the kitchen,' she said, 'And I'll make you a nice cup of tea.'

The room was reassuringly normal, just like a family kitchen, with oven, fridge, microwave and even kids' drawings pinned to a notice board. A darts board hung on an alcove wall. Evie sat down heavily on a wooden dining chair and watched as Mary filled the kettle and brought a bottle of milk from the fridge. She felt weak with exhaustion.

'There now,' said Mary, plonking the milky tea in front of her. 'Do you take sugar?'

'No, thanks.'

'Tell me, dearie, have you eaten anything today?'

Evie realised that she was ravenously hungry. 'No. No, I didn't have time for breakfast.'

'You must be starving, it's nearly lunchtime. I'll call the café and get them to deliver something for you. What would you fancy? A bacon roll, a square sausage roll? Toasted sandwich?'

'Oh, a sausage roll would be heaven. Thanks.'

'And a nice bit of flapjack for afters,' said Mary, comfortably. 'You'll be needing some sugar. You just sit and relax, I'll be back in a jiffy. The lavvy's just the next door along if you need to freshen up a bit.'

Then she was gone and Evie was alone. For the first time that day, she felt safe and protected. Her shoulders relaxed and she shut her eyes briefly, letting the silence fill her ears and calm her spirits. It was going to be OK now. She had done what she could. They would find Roddy now. Then she saw again the naked body, stretched out on the cold grave marker, the sheep tearing at the grass nearby, totally oblivious. Could she have saved Kayleigh? Why hadn't she recognised it was her from the vision? The blonde hair, the blue eyes, why hadn't she made the connection? What good was the vision if it hadn't been enough to save her? She could have warned Kayleigh not to go, to stay with the group. She began to cry, hot, slow tears coursing down her cheeks. She'd felt maternal towards her, protective, but the feeling hadn't been acute enough for her to realise the girl was in danger. It was the same with Marge and Brett. What good is it knowing they were in a cold, damp space surrounded by a curved wall? How was that supposed to help anyone locate them? Damn the flashes, damn then, she thought. They made me a smug, thoughtless little girl growing up, they ruined my marriage, and now they let three people I liked die. But another voice in her head said – but you got the killer, didn't you? That must count for something.

A tap on the door stopped her torturing herself. Mary entered the kitchen carrying a paper bag that smelt delicious. 'Here you go, dearie,' she said. 'You get stuck into that and you'll feel like a new woman. I'll be at the desk if you need anything, just give me a shout.'

***

It wasn't long until the door opened again and Fran stood there, pale and unusually dishevelled, as if she'd been hauled out of bed in a hurry. She wasn't wearing her customary mascara, and her short hair stuck up a little at the back. Evie threw herself into her sister's arms and clung to her. Fran rubbed her back, muttering small words of comfort, just as she had done when her sister was very small. Then they pulled apart and Fran said:

'Tell me what's happened.'

'Sit down. I'll tell you everything. But shall I make you a cup of tea first? You look like you could do with one.' She switched on the kettle and found a second mug.

'Yes, please,' said Fran. 'The policeman told me you were OK, but I got such a fright when he turned up at the door of my room. I thought... I thought you might be dead.'

Evie poured water on the tea bag, gave it a squeeze and added milk. She put the mug on the table and sat down opposite her sister.

'I could easily have been dead. Fran, it's Roddy. He killed them all.'

'Roddy? Our Roddy?'

'Yes.'

'I can't believe it!'

'It was Roddy. And the body that we found there at the church... that was Kayleigh.'

'No, oh no!' Fran was horrified, her face blanched in shock. She grasped Evie's hand across the table. 'But, it was... we only... Christ, we only saw her yesterday morning. That means...'

'Yes. She was killed sometime yesterday.'

'Oh my God. And then we actually asked Roddy for help. The same day he... Good God. I should never have let you go on your own. I'm so sorry!'

'It's my fault. I was determined to go.' Evie began to tell Fran everything that had happened since they had parted that morning. It felt like days ago to her, but it was just a few short hours. As she came to the end of her story, she saw Fran gawping at her, open-mouthed, shaking her head.

'He must be mad. Absolutely stark raving mad! And I sent you off in a car with him, with just a can of pepper spray. Jesus! Oh my God!'

'Well, thank God for the pepper pray. It saved my life!'

Fran had another thought. 'What would have happened if I'd have gone with you? Do you think he'd have tried to kill us both?'

'I don't think so. I don't think any of the murders were exactly pre-planned. He seems to kill on impulse, improvising and taking huge risks with a kind of blind faith that he won't get caught. If I hadn't seen the boots he'd have probably driven us both to the police station to report the murder, acting all innocent and concerned.'

Fran sipped her tea and Evie noticed that her hands were shaking.

'It's OK now, Fran. It's over. Or it will be soon. They'll catch him. What was happening at the hotel? Does anyone know anything there?'

'No, there were a couple of police cars there, but that's all I saw. I was in bed all morning.'

'Of course. How's your head now?'

'It's fine now. God, I still can't believe all this. It's too much. Tell me again? Slowly? How did he justify all the murders? Why did he agree to take you there?'

And so Evie went through the events of the morning once again to her sister. The act of recounting events for a fourth time was strangely calming. It had the effect of distancing Evie from things; as if she was recounting a scene from a film with a leading character that was nothing to do with her.

When the officers returned that afternoon, it became obvious that they had not managed to track down Roddy. They took Evie into an interview room to record her statement, and she was able to speak clearly and emotionlessly, giving more details and setting out the sequence of events with precision.

'There's something important that I forgot to mention this morning,' she said, as the interview drew to a close. 'I asked him if he was finished, if he was going to carry out another murder. And he is. He said he's planning to kill a cruise ship passenger.'

The two men looked at her with renewed attention. 'What else did he say? Did he tell you how he was going to do that?'

'He said he had a plan. But that's all. He didn't explain. I was trying to go along with it, as if I approved. I said it would be hard to separate a victim because they stick together in groups, but he didn't seem worried. He'd thought of a way, he said. He seemed excited about it.'

DS Sterling stopped the tape, then buzzed through to the other room. 'Dougie,' he said, 'I need the schedule for cruise ships coming into Portree for the next week. As quick as you can. Christ, this is a nightmare. We'll need to check each ship, check what excursions they have planned. Put one of our men on each bus. We'll have to call in more manpower from the mainland. Bloody hell!' He scratched his head, momentarily overwhelmed.

'This just doesn't happen here! It's unbelievable!'

'There haven't been any sightings of Roddy then?' asked Evie. 'No clue where he is now?'

'No. He probably hitched a lift. He could be anywhere.'

'Do you think he has an accomplice? That man, Arthur Ross, maybe he drove to pick him up. He knew about the victims' bodies. They could be working together.'

'No, we cleared him. He's no longer under suspicion. He told us he's writing some kind of book on pagan sacrifices. He'd managed to track down and interview the couple who found Florence Escoffier's body. That's how he knew how the body was displayed.'

'Oh, I see.' Still makes him a fucking weirdo, thought Evie. Creepy bastard.

The door opened and the policeman called Dougie came in with a sheaf of papers which he set down in front of the detectives.

'OK,' said DS Sterling, examining the papers. 'The Ocean Legend comes in at 8am tomorrow with three thousand passengers. And the Sea Vista comes in on Friday at 7am with one thousand two hundred. Then Monday next week we've got a smaller ship, the Silver Star, with seven hundred. We'll need to contact all the captains and get a list of the excursions.'

'Agreed. But some people don't book excursions, do they? They prefer to do their own thing. How can we keep those passengers safe?' asked his colleague with a worried frown. 'Should we cancel the dock? Ask the ships to go straight to the next port of call?'

'I'm not sure we've got the authority to do that. We can only inform the captains what the risk is. After that, it's their decision.'

'Agreed,' said Sergeant Reid. Then he turned back to Evie. 'Right, Mrs Carpenter, thank you so much for giving us your statement. Now we have to think how to keep you safe. Roderick

McAllister is still at large and you could be at risk. I don't want you or your sister going back to the Old Manse Hotel until we catch him.'

'Oh but... our things are there, and the art classes...'

'No, I'm afraid it's out of the question. We need you to lie low for a day or two, but stay somewhere where we can reach you if necessary. I'll get PC Carswell to find somewhere safe for you both. It shouldn't take too long; I think Mary knows every hotel and guest house on the island. We'll have you both settled before the end of the day.'

Evie returned to Fran in the kitchen, and filled the kettle again for tea.

'How did it go?' Fran asked.

'It went OK. I don't think I forgot anything. Bloody hell, I'm knackered though. Bone tired. They want to find us another place to stay though, they say we shouldn't go back to the Old Manse.'

'I guess that makes sense,' said Fran. 'He might look for you there.'

Evie shook her head. 'Do you think he'd risk coming after me a second time? I'm not so sure. I think he'll be after a cruise ship passenger next, like he told me.'

'Well, better safe than sorry. The police know best.'

Evie realised that she had been functioning on adrenaline for most of the day. All energy now left her. She felt completely drained and strangely numb. What the hell am I doing here, she thought. Did this morning really happen? It was all too incredible. The sisters lapsed into silence.

It was over an hour later, before Mary walked into the kitchen with Sergeant Reid. 'We've found alternative accommodation for you,' she said, with a hint of pride. 'It's on the isle of Raasay - that's the island you can see just across the bay from us here - so you'll be a ferry ride away from Skye, safe and sound, but still nice and close. We've booked a two-bed cottage on the main street – well, the only street, in the village of Inverarish. It's tiny. But there's a shop for provisions. I asked the owner to get you in some food and essentials for tonight – milk, eggs, bread, tea, that kind of thing, and you can get more shopping in the morning.' She beamed at them, and Sergeant Reid nodded his approval.

'So, Miss Lloyd,' he said to Fran, 'I've asked Sandy to take you back to the Old Manse so you can pack your things and your sister's things. Then once you're back here we'll take you over to the island in the police launch. Are you ready to go now?'

'Oh!' said Fran. 'Yes, yes I guess so!' She rose from her chair and went towards the door. Then she paused. 'But what about my car? It's at the hotel.'

'Leave it there for now. Leave the keys with us and we'll fetch it and bring it to the police station later.'

'Fran,' called Evie, as her sister was about to leave, 'If you see Aggie, can you tell her thanks. Thanks for all the classes. I really enjoyed them. Tell her I'm sorry about Roddy.' She paused and looked up at DS Reid questioningly. 'Will our art teacher know about Roddy? He's her friend's nephew, she must be upset.'

'Yes, she knows we're looking for him in connection to the murders. She's been interviewed.'

'Right. Oh, and Fran, can you say goodbye to Helen, if you bump into her. Tell her to keep on painting.'

'I will. See you soon, sis!'

Then, once more, Evie was left alone in the kitchen, alone with her thoughts. Tiredness overwhelmed her. She folded her arms on the table, let her head fall onto them, and was instantly asleep.

***

'Wake up sleeping beauty! Time to go!'

Fran was standing over her, in her green padded jacket and walking boots. Her enormous handbag was slung over her shoulder, and she held out Evie's own smaller bag. Evie blinked and shook out her arms, which had gone numb. Her neck cricked painfully as she straightened her spine. Then she stood up and followed her sister along the corridor to the front desk, where the two officers, Dougie and Sandy, were waiting with their wheeled suitcases. DS Sterling then marched into the reception area and started giving the officers instructions.

'We can't hang about,' he said. 'I want you to get these women down to the dock and onto the launch as quick as you can. We don't stop for anyone. When you get to the island it's a short walk. Do either of you know Inverarish?'

'I do,' said Dougie.

'Right. Then you know it's about a ten minute walk from the dock to the cottage on the main street. Get them settled in, then I want you both back here as quickly as possible. Got it?'

'Yes boss.'

DS Sterling turned to the sisters. 'The boat is literally two minutes walk away, at the harbour. I'll walk down with you. Have you both got your phones and your chargers?' They nodded. 'And you've got our phone numbers?' Again they nodded. 'Right then. Let's go.'

As DS Sterling opened the main door to the police station, looking out to check the coast was clear, Evie was suddenly overcome with fear. What if Roddy was out there, watching from a doorway? If he'd managed to find a lift, he'd know she'd go straight to the police. She felt exposed, terrified to leave the safety of the police station.

'I don't think I can...' she started.

'Come on, quick,' said DS Sterling, impatiently. 'Let's move!'

The five of them hurried out of the door and along the main street. It was six o'clock in the evening, but the street was still busy with passing cars and camper vans. Evie kept her head down, keeping as close as possible to DS Sterling's back. She felt the hairs at the base of her neck stand up. Am I being watched? Is he here? At the end of the street, just past a crowded café, they took a smaller, quieter road that dropped down to the shore, and at last saw the police boat waiting alongside a small pontoon. They walked down the metal gangplank and Dougie helped the sisters onto the vessel and to the seats at the rear, before disappearing into the cabin. DS Sterling looked around again, making sure they were not followed, then untied the ropes and threw them to Sandy on the boat. He waved briefly from the pontoon, as the engine started and the boat slowly edged away. Then, with a roar, the throttle opened and they were speeding away across the water.

The ride was short but exhilarating. Fresh, cold, salty air slammed in their faces as the powerful boat sliced through the water, sending up arcs of spray. Evie looked back at the Isle of Skye, the mountains still dominant and magnificent in the evening light, and felt a huge sense of relief to be leaving it behind. In no time at all they reached the island of Raasay, tiny compared to its neighbour, but rocky and rugged and wild. As soon as they disembarked and began walking along the pontoon towards the harbour, Evie was struck by the difference between the two islands. It was silent, apart from the cry of gulls and the gentle wash and rattle of water against the pebbly shore. Stacks of lobster pots, fishing ropes and plastic trays lined the harbour walls, giving off strong fishy smells. There were no people to be seen, no cars, just a scattering of low white houses on the wooded hill above. The only noise was the click-click of the suitcase wheels as Dougie and Sandy walked ahead of them up the narrow road. Sheep munched contentedly on the verges. A large bird, maybe an eagle, took off from the top branches of a tree. It was incredibly, powerfully tranquil.

'Beautiful, isn't it?' said Dougie, turning to the sisters with a smile. 'There's so much wildlife here. You'll see otters and red deer and sea eagles and golden eagles. And if you're lucky you can see dolphins in the bay.'

'How big is the island?' asked Fran.

'It's about eight miles long and a couple of miles across. You can walk everywhere in a day, you don't need a car here. In fact, there's not much point having a car, as there's only one road.'

Evie had a sudden insight into Roddy's twisted mindset. This was an island as it should be; full of raw nature, peaceful, traditional, and cherished and protected by the few inhabitants who called it home. This is what Roddy wanted for Skye. A kind of reclaiming of lost values. She found that she couldn't really blame him for that.

They soon came to a terrace of small whitewashed cottages with steep slate roofs, little windows and stone steps leading to the brightly painted front doors.

'Here we are,' said Dougie, walking up the steps of a neat, well-maintained cottage and opening the red door. 'This'll be your home for the next couple of days.'

The cottage felt instantly homely. The sitting room was decorated with chintzy wallpaper and the two deep sofas were adorned with tartan throws and cushions. Bookcases were set into the alcoves. Logs lay in the open fireplace which had a traditional tiled surround. Next door, the kitchen was small but well equipped. Fran opened the fridge and was relieved to see eggs, bacon, milk and a steak pie inside. A bottle of wine sat on the small table, next to a tin of baked beans and packet of home-made shortbread. The officers carried their suitcases up the narrow stairs to the bedrooms, then immediately came down again to say their goodbyes.

'That's us away now, then,' said Dougie. 'The wee shop's just a couple of doors down. It should have everything you need. The reception's good on Raasay, so keep your phones with you all the time. We'll be in touch every day.'

They thanked the officers and shut the door, locking it carefully and then double-checking the lock.

'I think this has been the longest day of my life,' said Evie. 'It's only just after seven o'clock and it feels like midnight.'

'Are you tired?' asked Fran. 'Do you want to go straight to bed?'

'No, I'm too wound up. I don't think I'd sleep. How are you? How's your head?'

'It's fine at the moment. Listen, let's try and have a super normal evening. Let's put the steak pie in the oven, pour ourselves a glass of wine and stick the TV on.'

They watched a series of old game shows on the Dave channel, sitting together on the sofa with their dinner on their laps, but Evie found it impossible to concentrate. The sounds and images from the TV washed over her like a mist, without penetrating her brain. Fran glanced over at her repeatedly, squeezing her hand and asking 'You OK?' but Evie just nodded and muttered 'Yep.'

Later, in the snug bedroom which sat under the sloping roof, Evie closed the curtains firmly, shutting out a fine sunset over the Cuillins of Skye. She undressed and got into bed with the covers pulled up to her chin. The bed was exquisitely comfortable. I'm safe, I'm safe here, she told herself. Safe and cosy and warm. But the minute she closed her eyes she felt again Roddy's hands around her neck, his thumbs pressing into her throat, and his beautiful golden eyes looking down at her with such pity and regret. Her own eyes shot open. It's just a memory, it's just a memory, she rationalised. It's not a premonition. He can't get you here, you're OK. You're safe.

Eventually, she fell into a deep, blissfully dreamless sleep.

CHAPTER FOURTEEN: RAASAY

Evie woke feeling alert and refreshed. She looked at her watch and was amazed to see that she'd slept for over ten hours. She wandered down the stairs in her pyjamas and found Fran in the kitchen, cup of tea in hand, looking at her phone.

'Morning!'

'Hi there. How did you sleep?' asked Fran.

'Like a log! Can't believe how long I slept! What about you. Any headaches?'

'No, thank God. I think the migraine episode may be finished. D'you want tea?'

'Ooh, yes.' Fran reached behind her and flicked down the knob so that the kettle began to sing again.

'What are you looking at?' asked Evie, pointing to Fran's phone with slight trepidation. She didn't want to think about death today, she didn't want to read the sensationalised headlines about Kayleigh, or speculate as to whether the press had connected the dots and realised they had a serial killer on the island.

Fran smiled. 'I've found a website about local walks. They all look fantastic. Are you up for a walk?'

'God, yes! Never more so!'

'Me too.'

Fran set the cup of tea on the table and began to read:

'This website is Five Great Walks on Raasay. The first one looks like it goes from the harbour, along the coast to a beach, then back through a forest.'

'Sounds great!'

'The next one goes through ancient woodland to the remains of a clearance village with ruined houses.'

'Not that one. Too sad.'

'Agreed. Number three goes to the top of the mountain we saw, and you get great views from the top, to Skye and also to the mainland. Sounds a bit steep though.'

'OK, next one?'

'This is the one for you, I think. You walk through ancient woodland to a bay where the royal family used to come with the royal yacht to picnic.'

'Ooh yes, I like the sound of that one!'

'Oh, wait, it's about three miles to the start of the walk. That'd be, what, eleven or twelve miles altogether. Bit too far maybe.'

'What's five?'

'The last one goes to a tidal island, you'd need to check the tide times, might be dodgy.'

'Let's do the first one. How long is it?'

'It says two and a half hours, about five miles.'

'Perfect. Shall we make a day of it, get picnic stuff from the shop? We can take it slow, sit on the beach and watch for otters.'

'Yes, let's. Breakfast first though. Fancy a bacon sarnie?'

Two hours later, the sisters set off. The weather was warm, with clear blue skies and a gentle breeze. They followed the road north towards the harbour, passing the impressive new whisky distillery, which they hadn't noticed the previous evening. Evie was momentarily struck again with sadness when she remembered that Marge and Brett had come here, and how much Brett had loved the young whisky. But the views to the west, over the sound towards the Trottenish coastline of Skye were breathtaking and she decided to shut out all negative thoughts today. Just above the harbour they noticed two huge statues on the hillside. They walked up to investigate, and found they were bizarre representations of mermaids, badly weathered and slightly sphynx-like, with the forearms extended out to the front, and the tail curled behind. Fran took a couple of photos, then they continued past the harbour and onto a grassy path that snaked over the headland, through groves of tangled rhododendrons before dropping down onto a sandy beach.

'Wow, it's so peaceful,' said Fran. 'Do you think there are otters here?'

'There might be some further up, where it gets more rocky.'

The sisters strolled along the deserted beach, soothed by the sound of the sea rippling onto the shore. At the far end, they sat on the bank above the rocks to watch for otters.

'Have you heard from Mum and Dad again?' asked Evie, in a whisper.

'No. I haven't told them about yesterday, or about where we are now. I didn't want to worry them. If they call us, we can fill them in. Have you heard from Jake again?'

'No. It didn't end too well when he phoned. I kind of implied that it was over between us.'

'Oh, Evie. You've got to talk to him, though. The girlfriend thing might have been a kneejerk reaction on his part. He might have dumped her, or maybe he feels bad about it, you never know. You've not had a real conversation with him, have you, since you moved out of the house?'

'No, not really. I suppose I'll have to have the conversation eventually. But tell me about you? How's your love life? You've always been a bit secretive about it!'

'Well, there's not much to tell; I have a friend I see now and again. We hook up for sex, or go to see a film or a play, or go out to eat.'

'Male friend or female friend?' asked Evie with a smile. She'd always wondered about this, but never found the right opportunity to ask. This quiet beach on an almost deserted island seemed to afford her the right moment.

Fran raised her eyebrows, shrugged, then gave a short laugh. 'I've tried both! But at the moment it's a girl friend.'

'That's great! I'm glad you've got someone.'

'Thanks. But I'm not like you. I don't need a partner. I like living on my own, not making compromises, pleasing myself. I'm not looking for a relationship, just a bit of companionship now and again. I suppose I might fall madly in love with someone one day, and have a change of heart, but at the moment I quite like the status quo.'

'I wish I was more like you. I'm crap at living on my own. I end up talking to the furniture!'

'Yeah, you always had a boyfriend in tow before you got married.' Fran gave Evie a searching look. 'Tell me, honestly, did you fancy Roddy a little bit? I mean, before you knew he was a psychopathic killer?'

'I suppose I did, a bit. I liked his hairy knees.'

Fran looked askance at Evie, and Evie stared back, as if to say 'so what?' then both sisters burst out laughing. Each time they caught each other's eye a fresh wave of laughter erupted. It was cathartic, cleansing, and Evie felt lighter than she had done for days.

'You're fucking mental,' said Fran, affectionately.

'I know,' grinned Evie. 'Well, that's scared off all the otters. Shall we get going again?'

The path continued northwards, between the rocky coastline and the wood above, then joined the single-track road for a few hundred metres, before veering off again into woodland. About a mile further on, they came to a signpost saying Temptation Hill, off to the right.

'Shall we try that?' asked Fran? 'Eat our picnic there?'

It was well worth the climb. The views out over the harbour and across to Skye were astonishing, as was the picnic bench, positioned just right to make the most of them. They unwrapped their sandwiches, opened their cans of Irn Bru, and ate in comfortable silence. They watched the ferry making its way across the dark blue water, back towards Skye.

'This is doing me so much good!' enthused Evie. 'I actually like this island even better than Skye. Do you realise, we haven't crossed paths with a single person, or seen a single car. It's so peaceful.'

'I know. I think we should come back here one day, when it's all over, and spend a week, do all the other walks on the website.'

'Yeah. I'd like that.'

The wind started to freshen and Fran pulled her coat tighter. 'Shall we make a move again? We've still got a way to go.'

They made their way back down the hill, and along the forest path before edging round a small loch. Here there was a signpost pointing the way to an iron-age broch, named Dun Borrofiach.

'Do you want to walk up to see the broch, or will it make you think of where they found Marge and Brett?' asked Fran.

'No, let's give it a go. I've never seen one before. I'm not really sure what they are.'

'Oh, I looked it up the other day. They were roundhouses, probably built by the Picts as a defence against the Scots. They're over two thousand years old.'

The broch stood on the crest of a hill, in a clearing in the forest. It was a tumble of deep green, moss-covered stones, in a vaguely circular mound, but was in a lamentable state of preservation. Again, though, the view from the clearing was staggering. It was easy to imagine how the broch would have had an ideal defensive position, looking out, as it did, in all directions. As they admired it, a group of three red deer emerged from the forest and walked calmly across the clearing, seemingly unperturbed by their presence.

'Magical' breathed Evie, as the deer re-entered the forest. 'Just magical.'

**

It was late afternoon by the time the sisters reached the cottage in Inverarish.

'Well,' said Evie, taking off her coat and walking boots in the entrance, 'that has been a surprisingly, thoroughly enjoyable day!'

'It has,' agreed Fran. 'You know, I never do this kind of thing. I never slow down, look at nature, pause and just appreciate stuff around me. My London life is great, but it's so full-on. I must plan days like this more often. It's good for the soul. So what do you want to do now?'

'Um, how about we take a glass of wine and sit in the little garden outside? It's a real sun trap. I'd love to see your photos.'

Both sisters had paused frequently on the walk to take phone shots. Fran had a better eye for composition, and Evie was hoping to pinch a few that she could use later for her own sketches. They had both checked their phones for messages during the walk, but there had been nothing from the police. They had deliberately avoided looking at their newspaper apps all day.

They sat at the wooden table in the late afternoon sunshine, glass in hand, sending each other photos on WhatsApp, then did an online crossword together.

'Do you do Wordle?' asked Evie, when they'd found the last clue.

'No, I've never had the time really, life's so busy. Everyone talks about it. Is it good?'

'Yeah, it's fun. I used to do lots of quizzes. I've let them drop a bit recently. Here, I'll show you.'

The sisters then competed to complete Wordle and Quiz of the Day. The time passed pleasantly, until the sun began to lose its warmth and the sisters adjourned to the kitchen to start making dinner. Evie found herself humming as she separated a string of sausages and lay them on the grill pan. And then her ringtone sounded and she snatched up her phone.

'Police' she mouthed at Fran, as she pressed the accept call icon.

'Yes. Yes, we're both fine... No... So have you found... Nothing? Oh... OK.' There was a long pause as Evie listened. Her face became worried and Fran strained to catch the words, but could hear little. 'Oh, oh no! O God... No, I haven't seen or felt anything, I'm sorry. Yes, yes I will, of course. Yes. OK, yes, right. Thanks. Goodbye.'

Evie replaced the phone on the table and looked at Fran. Her face left little doubt that there was bad news.

'There's a cruise ship passenger gone missing,' said Evie. 'They were all supposed to be back on the ship at five o'clock, and the ship has had to leave without one person. A fifty year-old man from Reading.'

'But it doesn't mean necessarily... I mean, you hear about people missing the ship deadline and being left behind, don't you?'

'Yes, it happens. But the police are taking it seriously. They're searching the churchyards and ruins all over Skye.'

'No sightings of Roddy?'

'None.'

'Oh shit. But you haven't had any flashes today?'

'Not a thing.'

'Well, maybe it's not related. Maybe the cruise ship guy just lost track of time, fell asleep somewhere... or had an accident.'

'Let's hope so. I'm going to try not to think about it. It's been such a good day. I don't want to ruin it.'

'Agreed. Get the sausages under the grill and I'll peel the potatoes for mash.'

The evening passed peacefully, with both sisters sitting in the kitchen where the lights were brightest, sketching island views from Fran's phone photos, before adding colour washes.

Once tucked up in the comfortable bed, Evie felt fairly relaxed. There had been no visions, no feelings of fear or loss. Maybe whatever had happened to that man was nothing at all to do with Roddy McAllister, she thought, as she fluffed up her pillow and switched off the bedside light.

Seconds later, she was fast asleep.

CHAPTER FIFTEEN: THE DISTILLERY

'Knock, knock!'

Evie stirred as she heard her sister's voice. Then the door was pushed open and Fran backed into the room, bearing two cups of tea. She put one on the bedside table, then sat down on the edge of the bed.

'What time is it? asked Evie, her voice still hoarse with sleep.

'Nearly nine o'clock. Did you have a good night?'

'Yes, I did.' Evie pulled herself upright against the padded headrest and picked up her mug. 'Perfectly dreamless sleep. Wonderful. What about you?'

'I slept well too. It must be all the fresh air we had yesterday. No visions?'

'Nothing.'

'Good! Then what should we do today?'

'Um, I wouldn't mind another walk. Maybe find another beach and watch for otters again? But you choose.'

'That suits me fine! It looks like another beautiful day.'

'What day is it today? I've lost count.'

'It's Thursday the eighteenth. We're on day nine of what was supposed to be our ten-day painting holiday. We'd have been going home tomorrow.'

'God. You know, it all feels like ages ago that we did the workshop. It feels like that was a completely different time and place, as if we've been teleported into a different time zone somehow.'

'I know what you mean. It's so nice here. Like a different world.'

'What about your job? When are you supposed to be back?' asked Evie.

'Not till Monday. But I can extend it if the police need us to stay.' Fran gave Evie a sheepish look. 'I know we weren't going to, but I did check my phone this morning, just in case. There was nothing about a new body. I thought you'd like to know that.'

'Oh, right, thanks. That's a relief. Was there lots about the other murders? About Kayleigh?'

'Yes, but I didn't read past the headlines. They looked pretty sensationalist. They're calling him the 'Son of Satan.' You know, serial killer on the loose, pagan sacrifices...'

'God. That's just what Roddy hoped for. Stupid name though. I don't think pagans are anything to do with devil worshippers. I wonder if people are cancelling their bookings, like he thought?'

'I bet they are. Three murders, maybe that would make you think twice, but three supposedly satanic murders, I think I'd probably cancel. Anyway, enough of that. We've got another lovely day ahead of us. Let's get breakfast started.'

Fran scrolled down her phone, looking for information on wildlife as they ate their bacon and egg rolls in the kitchen.

'Listen to this,' she said. 'Otters are commonly found on the shores near Fearns Beach at Suisnish. That's just near here, in the opposite direction from yesterday, but not far at all to walk. And it says there's wonderful birdlife too: oystercatchers, curlews, cormorants. And seals too. And maybe even dolphins!'

'That sounds heavenly! Right, I'll make the sandwiches and boil some eggs.'

Shortly thereafter, the sisters pulled on their walking boots, zipped up their padded jackets and set out south, following the single-track road as it hugged the rocky shoreline. The beaches here were narrow and pebbly, and strewn with orangey-green kelp. Large and small rocks littered the shore and were also scattered in the shallow waters, which were a clear translucent turquoise. Wading birds scuttled about at the water's edge and a couple of cormorants stretched out their wings to dry on a rock further out. The Black Cuillins were shining indigo and purple beyond the water, and they could easily make out individual houses on the opposite shoreline of Skye. The sisters sat in silence on the grass above the beach, drinking in the sights and hoping for something special.

After about half an hour, Evie spotted a slight movement in the kelp behind some rocks, at the point where the waves reached the shore. She nudged Fran and pointed to the spot, where it seemed that something brown was see-sawing back and forth. There was no wind today, so that did not account for the movement. They continued to watch for minutes, and Fran silently pulled out her phone and zoomed in on the shape.

'I think it's an otter,' she whispered. 'It's his back. I think he might be gnawing at a fish or something.'

'Oh wow! Do you think it really is?'

At that moment, the creature paused, then raised its head to look directly at them. The beady black eyes held theirs for an instant. They saw its sleek, wet fur, its long whiskers and prominent nostrils. The remains of a fish dangled from its jaws. One paw was raised, poised for flight. The creature sniffed the air, then in one quick motion turned and disappeared into the water. They tried to follow its path, but it had disappeared.

'Incredible!' said Evie. 'We're so lucky!'

'And look,' said Fran, showing her the phone. 'I've caught him on camera!'

The photo was pixelated, but it was quite clearly an otter. Evie laughed, delighted. 'We're not going to beat that! Unless we see a basking shark or something! Where shall we go next?'

'I think if you follow the road to the tip of the island, there looks like a footpath across the moors back to Inverarish. Shall we do that?'

'Let's go!'

They met no-one on the narrow road south, apart from sheep. As the road turned around the southern tip of the island, the views changed, and they found themselves staring at the gentler, aptly named flanks of the Red Cuillins. The road petered out at the tiny hamlet of Eyre, and they easily found the long, straight footpath leading back through the bracken to Inverarish.

They were over halfway along this path, with home almost in sight, when Evie suddenly stopped.

Fran looked back, puzzled. Evie had closed her eyes and was breathing fast. One hand was placed over her chest.

'What is it?' asked Fran, sounding worried. 'What's wrong?'

'He's here.'

'What d'you mean? Roddy?'

'Yes. He's getting off the ferry. He's wearing a black beanie hat, I can't see his hair, but I'm sure it's him!'

'Oh shit, oh shit!'

'I don't know whether this is now, or in the future. I can't tell.'

'We need to get safe. I'm calling the police.'

Fran got out her mobile and found the number that she'd already saved to her contacts. She pressed the call icon but the phone rang and rang. The sisters looked at each other in alarm.

'Come on, come on!' Evie hopped from foot to foot, panic gnawing at her. She could hear the blood thundering in her ears. Her chest felt tight. 'Fuck sake! Answer, please!'

Fran stopped the call, then tried once more. Again it rang and rang. At last Fran spoke:

'Hello, I need to speak to Sergeant Reid or DS Sterling. It's urgent.... Fran Lloyd...' There was a pause. Fran glanced up at

Evie, and grabbed her arm to reassure her. 'It's Fran Lloyd. My sister has had a premonition. Roddy is here, on the island of Raasay. Yes, she's sure... Yes... Yes, I know where that is. Yes, OK. Yes, we'll go now.'

Fran stopped the call and put the phone in her pocket. She took hold of Evie's shoulders, to stop her shaking.

'That was DS Sterling. He's coming over right now with two officers on the launch. They'll be here soon. He said we should get to some place where there are people and wait there. He said the best place would be the distillery. There's a bar there, and a restaurant, it should be full of people. He'll meet us there.'

Evie was still struggling to breathe and Fran knew she was on the edge of a full panic attack. She spoke calmly:

'Keep it together Evie,' she said. 'Breathe in... and out...in... and out... Think about the otter. Think about the deer yesterday. OK? In... and out...'

She continued the count until Evie's heart stopped its mad racing and her breath became less ragged.

'Right. Do you think you can walk again now?'

'Yes, I think so.'

'OK. Good. Have you still got the pepper spray?'

Evie felt in her jacket pocket. 'No, she wailed. 'It's not there! I must have... Oh fuck, I left it on the table in the kitchen.' She began to tremble again.

'It's OK, we'll be OK. But we have to go now. It's not far, we'll be there in a few minutes. Come on.'

The two women walked as fast as they were able, soon reaching the little village, then taking the road down towards the harbour. They saw the ferry in the distance, making its way back to Sconser.

'I don't like this,' said Evie. 'The distillery is the first place you see from the harbour. Won't he look there first? What if he sees us going in?'

'We've got to go there, that's where the police will come. It'll be safe there. Come on, we're nearly there.'

They ran the last few hundred metres. The distillery car park was reassuringly full. Thank God, thought Fran, it's still open. There are people.

'Shit,' panted Evie, as they ran up the path. 'Which building is the bar in?'

The distillery consisted of a brand new glass-fronted visitor centre, and a stone-built Victorian hotel. The two buildings were connected by a large, ultra-modern gold-coloured cube.

'That must be the reception, I think,' said Fran, pointing at the gold cube. 'It's probably in that part. Come on!'

They ran past the surprised woman at the reception desk, past the shop and pushed open the door of the tasting bar, catching their breath. The bar was beautiful; fresh and modern, with a clean wooden floor, round tables and comfortably upholstered chairs in tasteful pastel colours, but it was disappointingly empty. A well-dressed elderly couple sat at one table, eating a snack and chatting. Evie and Fran were aware of their own shabby appearance. Their jeans were dirty from sitting on the grass, they were both sweaty and red in the face. Fran straightened her spine, ran a hand through her short hair and pulled Evie towards the sleek wooden bar. The young barman in his purple distillery polo shirt smiled at them without judgement.

'What can I get you?'

'Two whiskies please,' said Fran, fishing in her pocket for her credit card.

The barman proceeded to reel off a list of various whisky choices but Fran wasn't really listening.

'Oh, just the first one, please,' she said. The barman measured out the drinks, and as he turned away, she held out a glass to Evie and whispered: 'Where should we sit? Where's safest? By the window to watch for the police coming, or by the door to make a quick exit, or in the back bit there?'

'Not the window. Over there,' said Evie, pointing to a table at the far end of the curved bar.

'Drink. It'll calm our nerves,' said Fran as they sat, both facing the door with their backs to the wall.

Evie lifted her glass with a shaking hand and took a gulp. Then she looked at Fran.

'He's coming. He's really near. I can feel it. What do we do if he comes in here?'

'We keep calm. We keep him talking. The police have got to get here soon. It didn't take us long to get across the water, they'll be here soon.'

Evie's breath was coming in shallow jerks again and Fran knew another panic attack was imminent. 'Evie, look at me. Deep breath in... then out... in... then out. Remember the five things method. Close your eyes. Now, what can you hear?'

'The old couple's knives and forks clinking.'

'Good, good. What can you smell?'

'Distillery smells. Barley, whisky, peaty smells.'

'What can you feel?'

'The glass, the chair beneath my bum.'

'Good. And what can you see?'

'The door opening and... Oh fuck, oh fuck, I see Roddy...'

Evie's eyes shot open. And there he was, large as life, coming towards them and smiling as if it was a genuine pleasure to see them again. The sisters froze. Evie's heart was pounding faster and her fingers began to tingle.

'Hello ladies,' he said, pulling off his black beanie hat and revealing his rust-brown hair. He sat down opposite them at the small table and relaxed back in his seat, totally at ease. He unzipped his jacket and raised a hand towards the barman.

'Can I get whatever the girls are having?' he asked, his voice warm and natural.

'Right away,' said the barman. He brought the drink to the table.

Neither sister spoke. Instead they watched Roddy, their bodies tense with fear. Roddy took a sip of his whisky and nodded his approval. 'Oh, that's some good stuff!' he said, conversationally.

Evie fought to control her nerves. We have to keep him talking, she thought. As calmly as she was able, she spoke:

'Hello Roddy. How did you find us?'

'Och, that was easy. I saw you getting on the polis boat and I thought you'd be coming across the water to Raasay. So I got the ferry over just now, and as luck would have it, there you both were, hurrying up to the distillery.' He smiled, genial and at ease. This was the Roddy they knew from the hotel, calm and friendly, so deceptive. Evie forced herself to smile back at him.

'So did you get your cruise ship passenger yesterday?' she asked.

'Yes, I did indeed. My wee plan worked out just fine.'

'What was your plan? I'm intrigued.' Keep him talking! Keep him talking! Evie's hand reached under the table to grasp Fran's hand. She gave it a squeeze.

'The only hitch was having to steal a car – thanks to you! But the rest went just as I hoped. When the excursion buses had left the dock, some foot passengers got off to have a wander round Portree. I knew they would. I accidentally-on-purpose bumped into one of them, apologised, and we got chatting. Nice man, very friendly. I asked him about his family, where he was from, and where the cruise was heading next. Then I asked what kind of shop he wanted to find in Portree – whisky shop, wool shop, gift shop? And he said he wanted to buy a knitted sweater for his wife. Oh, I said, there's a sale on in a warehouse just outside town. I'm going that way, I can give you a lift. You see how easy it is? Everyone trusts a Highlander, it seems.'

'Where did you leave the body?' asked Fran.

'At Borreraig. It's a ruined clearance village, way up north. It'll take them a while to find it.'

'Did you display the body in the same way?' asked Evie.

'Of course!' Roddy grinned. 'I have to keep up the game. I took off his shirt and crossed his arms, took off the shoes and laid them by his side.'

'So is that the end now? Are you done?'

'No, there's one more. And I'm thinking maybe a camper van too. But I'll wait a wee while for that one. The press are all over Skye just now, it's brilliant.'

Evie hardly dared ask the next question. 'And why are you here, now, why did you come to find us?'

'Well now,' said Roddy, and suddenly his face changed. The smile disappeared and his eyes had that strange, excited gleam again. 'You disappointed me, Evie. I thought you were on my side.'

'I got scared! But I do understand what you're doing, really.'

'You went to the polis, did you not? You gave them my name. It's going to be a lot harder for me to continue now. I'm a wee bit fashed about that.'

'I... I'm sorry, I...'

'So you see, I thought I'd do one more today.' Roddy searched in his pocket and pulled out his sgian dubh, his short dagger. He placed his fist, gripping the handle, on the table, then covered the exposed blade with his other hand. Evie glanced up at the barman, but he was not looking their way. No-one had seen anything. She gripped Fran's hand tighter, terrified.

'But I canna decide which one of you to kill,' Roddy continued in his easy, conversational voice. 'I'm getting the ferry back in ...' here he twisted his wrist slightly to look at his watch, 'in fifteen minutes. I reckon I can do one of you, and be out of here and onto the ferry before anyone notices.'

'You'll never get away with that. People will see! They'll stop you at the ferry!'

'Och, I don't think so. My luck has held this far. But which one?' He looked from one sister to the other, slowly, a smile playing on his lips. Then he began to tap the blade of the dagger on the table. Tap, tap, tap. 'I'll just stick the knife in, under the ribs, give it a wee twist. You won't feel much pain. It'll be quick and there won't be much blood. I'll be away to the ferry before you're even dead.'

Evie felt Fran drop her hand, then thump her sharply on the knee. She looked down. She saw Fran's hand reach towards the edge of the table, then her fingers sign 'one, two, three' and then both hands miming a push. Evie understood immediately. Fran's fingers once more signed one, two, three, then Evie and Fran simultaneously pressed the heels of their palms against the table edge and shoved it with all the strength they could muster. The table slammed into Roddy's solar plexus. His chair fell backwards with a crash. The knife flew out of Roddy's hand and skidded across the polished wooden floor. Roddy scrambled to his knees, winded, but Evie was faster. She shot out of her chair and grabbed the knife as it came to rest against the base of the bar. As Roddy started to stand up, she held it towards him with a shaking hand.

Evie was aware of the elderly couple leaving their seats and moving away. The woman was saying 'oh, oh, oh!' over and over. Out of the corner of one eye, she saw the barman reach for a phone on the wall behind him and speak into it. Fran had left her seat and had come to stand behind her.

Roddy got to his feet slowly, and took one step towards Evie. He held out one hand, placatingly. 'You're not going to use that, now, are you, lassie?' he said in his smoothest, most calming voice. 'I don't think you've got it in you, have you?'

Evie jerked the dagger towards him, and he lifted both his

hands in defence.

'Give me the dagger, Evie,' he said. 'It's my dagger, my sgian dubh. It belonged to my father.' He took another step. 'I'd hate to lose it.' Another step.

'Don't come closer. I'll stab you!' said Evie in a shaky voice.

'Och, I don't think so,' said Roddy. Another step. 'You couldn't do it, could you? You've got a soft heart.' His hand was now just inches away from Evie's fist.

Evie now saw, behind Roddy, that two burly, purple-shirted distillery workers had entered the bar. Their arms were huge and muscled, and for one bizarre moment Evie imagined them tossing whisky barrels onto a truck. They stood in the doorway, assessing the scene. The larger, bearded one spoke:

'Drop the knife, now, lassie!'

Fran put her hand over Evie's to press the knife more firmly into her grasp. She said in a strong, clear voice: 'This man is Roderick McAllister. He's wanted for the murder of five tourists on Skye. The police are on their way.'

Roddy looked around. He saw the two thickset distillery workers coming towards him. He laughed. 'She's nuts,' he said, his voice higher than usual. 'They're both nuts, I'm not that man!'

But the two workers continued to advance slowly towards him. Roddy suddenly span away and made to sprint past them, but he was caught on the arm by the first man. Then, as they struggled, the second lifted a bottle of whisky from a wooden display box on the wall and sent it smashing into the back of Roddy's head. Roddy fell heavily against the bar, momentarily stunned, but then righted himself, lashing out with a strength born of desperation. He landed a hard punch on the bearded man, but two against one was proving too much. He was eventually tackled to the ground and yanked onto his stomach, his head pressed hard into the wooden floor. The second man sat on his legs and pulled his hands together, yelling to the barman:

'Fling us a cloth or something, Pete. We'll tie his hands.'

As Roddy struggled, the barman dipped a tea towel in the sink, wrung it out quickly and threw it over. Roddy's hands were securely tied. The bearded man lifted him up and forced him onto a chair. All fight suddenly seemed to go out of Roddy. He sat calmly, deflated, looking down at his feet.

'Lucky the bottle didn't break,' said the bearded man laconically, retrieving the whisky and replacing it in the display box on the wall. He grinned.

Evie laid the dagger on the bar and collapsed against Fran. She was shaking uncontrollably.

'You say the police are on their way?' asked the bearded man.

'Yes, we called them about half an hour ago. They're coming over from Portree in the launch,' said Fran.

'OK then, so we'll wait a wee while with our friend here.' He put a meaty restraining hand on Roddy's shoulder.

Roddy looked up and smiled meekly about the room. He smiled at the elderly couple, still shocked and shaking. He smiled at the two distillery workers, and he smiled at Evie and Fran.

'Well, that's that, I suppose. The game's a bogey now,' he said, quietly. Then, as he continued to speak, his voice took on a stronger, more assured tone. 'But I did what I had to do. I've saved the island from mass tourism. Less people will want to come now. The locals can get their houses back, their roads back, their beauty spots back. Less pollution, less camper vans, less cruise ships. When I go to trial I'll tell everyone what I did and why I did it. They'll thank me. I'll be a folk hero. I'll be mentioned in the same breath as the Bonnie Prince, as Robert the Bruce and William Wallace. The man who fought for his land, against an army of invaders. That's me! They'll write books about me!' He pronounced this last sentence fiercely, his eyes alive with passion, just like a minister at the pulpit, preaching fire and brimstone to the flock.

'You're deluded,' said Evie, scornfully. 'You killed five people and you expect a round of applause? It's not going to happen.' But she wondered if what he said was true. There was always such a morbid fascination with serial killers. There were bound to be books written, interviews given, maybe a TV documentary made. He would become famous. But had he 'saved Skye?' She thought, perversely, that his actions might have the opposite effect. Skye would become even more well-known. More tourists would come. There would be 'Son of Satan' tours, trips to all the sites where bodies had been discovered, just like the Ripper Tours in London. Roddy would languish in some grey city prison, far from his homeland, with no mountain views, no fresh sea air, and realise that it had all been for nothing. She looked at Roddy's glowing face, and, just for an instant, felt a little sorry for him. Then she remembered Kayleigh's lifeless body, and all pity vanished.

Within minutes, DS Sterling appeared in the doorway, with Sandy and Dougie just behind. They quickly assessed the scene.

'Cuff him, Dougie,' said DS Sterling, and the tea towel was replaced by metal handcuffs. Roddy sat, still smiling, as DS Sterling towered over him. All his former bravado had disappeared and he now looked innocent and bemused, like a schoolboy being told off by a headmaster.

'Roderick McAllister, you are under arrest for the murders of Florence Escoffier, Marjorie Carter, Brett Carter and Kayleigh Petersen, and on suspicion of the murder of Philip Arnott. You do not have to say anything, but it may harm your defence if you do not mention when questioned something which you later rely on...'

It seemed extraordinary to Evie to hear the words that she had heard so often in police dramas on TV. Suddenly the whole day seemed unreal. Her legs felt weak and she sat down.

DS Sterling then came over to the sisters. His eyes took in

the fallen chair and the three whisky glasses on the floor, one of which had smashed. He saw the knife on the bar, and the girls' numb faces.

'Are either of you hurt?' he asked.

'No, we're OK. He said he was going to kill one of us,' said Fran.

'We should get you to Portree and get you both to a doctor.'

'No, honestly, we're fine,' said Evie. 'It's just shock. We'd rather stay here.' If Roddy was going to be taken away, she didn't want to be on the same boat as him. She knew his calm, pleasant demeanour could switch in a heartbeat to reckless violence, and she didn't want to be anywhere near him.

'I insist. You need a check-up.' He paused. 'OK, tell you what, I'll see if someone from the Portree medical centre can come over on the next ferry to examine you.' He moved away a couple of metres and spoke into his radio. 'Mary, get the cell ready. We're coming over with the suspect. And can you ask one of the medics from the centre to get over to Raasay on the next ferry? ...Yes... The distillery... OK... All under control.'

He returned to the sisters. 'We'll need to get statements from you both, and from everyone in the bar.' His gaze took in the elderly couple and the distillery workers. 'But we'll do that tomorrow. Sandy, can you get everyone's names and phone numbers please?'

He turned again to Evie and Fran. 'Can you both stay here until the doctor arrives?'

'We'll take care of the lassies,' said the bearded man. 'They've had a rough time of it. We'll get them something to eat and drink, and make sure they're OK till he gets here.'

'Very good,' said DS Sterling. He turned again to Roddy, who was still sitting quietly in his chair, watching the exchange with interest. 'On your feet, McAllister. Time to go.'

'Oh,' said Evie, as the officers prepared to leave. 'He told us where the latest body is. The cruise ship man. It's at a clearance village right up north. I can't remember the name. Something beginning with 'B', I think.'

'Is that so?'

'Yes,' said Roddy, helpfully. 'He's in Borreraig, just past Dunvegan. I can show you exactly where he is.'

DS Sterling took his radio out again. 'Mary, get the search to head up to Borreraig. It's on the west shores of Loch Dunvegan.' He replaced his radio and said to Roddy: 'You're going straight to the cells, my lad.'

The three officers lifted Roddy from his seat and escorted him out of the building. Everyone watched from the tall windows as the party made their way down to the harbour, with Dougie and Sandy each holding one of Roddy's arms.

Evie then turned to the two distillery workers. 'I don't know how to thank you both! And you too,' she said to the barman. 'You all saved our lives! What are your names? We need to thank you properly.'

'I'm Hamish and this here's Andrew,' said the bearded one. 'Pete's behind the bar. But it looked like you had the situation well under control to me. You were the one holding the knife!'

'Yes, but he knew I couldn't use it.'

'The important thing is, we got the bastard. Between us we got the bastard. These murders – they have no place on our islands.'

More distillery workers and visitors now crowded into the bar, intrigued to know what was going on, and why the police had been there. The atmosphere became almost festive, with whisky poured all round, and excited conversations taking place, as Hamish, Andrew, Pete and the elderly couple recounted what had happened to the astonished onlookers. Evie and Fran sat at the table sipping their whisky and watched, emotionally spent, numb. It took a long time before the distillery staff went back to their tasks and the visitors returned to the car park, or walked off in the direction of the harbour. Finally, just a handful of people remained in the bar.

Pete the barman came over to the sisters. 'Whereabouts are you staying?'

'At the cottage in Inverarish,' said Fran.

'I'll walk you back up there, after the doctor's been, if you like.'

'That's kind of you,' said Fran, 'but I think we're alright now. The danger is over. But is it ok if we eat our picnic in here?' She lifted the small bag that contained their sandwiches and boiled eggs, and placed it on the table. It looked a bit squashed and Pete eyed it dubiously.

'No, I think not,' he said. He turned and fetched something from the bar. 'We can do better than that. Here's the snack menu. Pick what you like, on the house. You've probably got time before the ferry comes in.'

***

It was late afternoon before Evie and Fran finally returned to the cottage. The doctor had declared them physically in good health, but warned them of the consequences of shock.

'You've both experienced trauma,' she'd said. 'There might be some physical symptoms that occur, like breathlessness, light-headedness. That's normal. Your emotions are also probably all over the place. You might feel a rush of different emotions, like numbness, rage or anger. You might find yourself just sitting there, not able to do anything. Or you might have a sense of unreality. All that is normal. What you need to do is sleep, rest, find a nice safe place where you feel comfortable, and just give yourself the time to adjust. It's good that you're together, but don't try and talk things through too soon. Just let things lie for a while. I don't recommend you do anything stressful for a few days. Just take it easy. If these feelings persist, then you will need to speak to a professional, someone who deals with PTSD.'

'I know the doctor said don't talk things through,' said Evie, as they had walked back towards the cottage. 'But I can't help wondering which one of us he was going to kill. If anything had happened to you, I wouldn't have been able to… well, just… You've always been…Shit. What I'm trying to say, I guess, is thank you, Fran. You've always been there for me. Always.'

'That's what sisters are for, idiot,' said Fran. 'We look out for each other. So what do you want to do next? We've got to give statements tomorrow, but after that? Do you feel like you want to go straight home to Yorkshire? Back to your flat, or to mum and dad's? Or stay here? It's Thursday now, but we could stay till Sunday, if you like? Or longer? I can easily get a few more days off.'

'I think I'd rather stay here for a few days. It's so peaceful and quiet. Just to be with you, no need to explain or talk. Just walk, eat, watch TV, just zone out. Once we get back home … ugh, I can't think about being back in the flat. And all the questions our parents are going to ask… I haven't got the energy to deal with that right now. Is it ok with you if we stay here? At least till Sunday?'

'Of course! That's what I'd rather do too. Now, let's get a couple of pizzas and a bottle of wine from the shop, find some mindless TV to watch, and forget about everything.'

C HAPTER SIXTEEN: AFTERMATH

Evie and Fran didn't have the energy to do very much at all the next day. They had both had a poor night, with interrupted sleep. Evie had woken up at three in the morning, soaked in sweat, after a dream in which the dagger had been thrust into Fran's body. In her dream, Evie had attempted to stem the flow of blood with the palms of her hands, but the sticky liquid oozed relentlessly between her fingers, staining her hands red. She had screamed as Fran crumpled in on herself and deflated like a burst balloon, becoming smaller and smaller until she had completely disappeared. All that remained was the blood on Evie's hands. She had woken in a panic, heart pounding, clammy with sweat. She put the bedside light on and tried to slow her breathing. It's just a dream, just a dream, she told herself. She checked her hands. Clean, no blood, of course. What did you expect? Everything is OK now. Fran's OK, sleeping soundly in the next bedroom. She tried to empty her mind, to be calm, but the bad thoughts whirred and crashed and danced repeatedly in her brain like spiteful dervishes.

It was a while before she dropped off to sleep again. The next dream was just as bad. She saw the abandoned church on the rocky ridge, swathed in mist. A body was lying on a grave marker. A scattering of crows were pecking at it and Evie ran, clapping her hands, to scare them off. They watched her approach with beady eyes, then at the last minute flapped off to perch on top of the stone wall, following her movement with jerks of their heads, cawing angrily. When Evie reached the body she looked down and realised it was herself lying there, naked, with hands crossed over her chest and eyes wide open. She woke with a start, once again shivering and damp with sweat. She realised sleep was impossible. She reached for one of the books sitting in the little alcove above the bed, a light romance, and tried unsuccessfully to immerse herself in the story, but it was no good. Finally, at about six o'clock, she gave up and went downstairs, to find Fran sitting at the kitchen table, also in her pyjamas. Her eyes had dark shadows beneath, and her hair was sticking up at the front.

'Hi! You look as rough as I feel,' said Evie. 'Bad night?'

'Yep, I had a nightmare, pretty crappy.'

'Me too. What was yours?'

'I dreamt that I was driving us back south, at night, you and me in the front seats, and then I looked in the mirror and saw that Roddy was in the back seat, smiling at us. Just smiling his friendly smile, but it was so creepy. Then I woke up.'

'Mine was worse. I dreamt you were dead. Bloody hell! Do you think we've got PTSD?'

'Maybe, a bit. But it's good we've both been through the same thing. We can work through it together. Cup of tea?'

'Oh, yes please.'

Fran got up to refill the kettle and fetch a mug from the cupboard. 'I looked at the news headlines on my phone,' she said. 'They talk about a thirty-seven year-old man being arrested in connection with five murders on Skye, but they don't go into any details about him. They rehash the previous murders again, and there's a lot about the cruise ship man, too.'

'We're not mentioned at all?'

'Not a thing.'

'That's good. Maybe we'll be kept out of it. Hope so. I don't want our names in the papers.'

'Want some breakfast?' asked Fran.

'Yeah, I do actually. I'm pretty hungry. Shall we do a fry-up?'

The sisters spent a very quiet morning in the cottage, making a conscious effort to avoid talking about the murders. They wandered round to the little shop and bought a handful of trashy gossip magazines and a book of easy crosswords. They had edged past the newspaper display, trying not to look at the headlines, but Evie had caught a glimpse of a fuzzy black and white shot of a man being escorted inside a police station by two officers. Good, she thought, it's real. He's in a cell. They took their haul of magazines out into the small front garden with a cup of coffee, amusing themselves with the personality quizzes – 'Which Madonna are you?' and 'Which British Queen would have been your best friend?' They laughed at the celebrity gossip and sniggered at the horoscopes: 'Your ambitious nature will bring you great success this week, but remember to wear your lucky socks (Fran, Aries) and 'Expect some dramatic truth-telling this week, as you wrestle with what recent events mean for your relationship (Evie, Scorpio).

The day wore on peacefully enough, until late afternoon, when the police arrived. This time it was Sergeant Reid who drove the police car, and Evie was relieved to see the friendlier, more paternal officer. He was closely followed by Sandy, who parked Fran's blue BMW outside the cottage. They made more cups of tea, then Evie stayed in the living room while Fran gave and signed her statement in the kitchen. It only took about twenty minutes. And then it was her turn.

'First of all, how are you?' asked Sergeant Reid as they sat down. As Evie looked into his kind eyes, she was aware of Sandy fiddling with some equipment just off to his right.

'Oh, not too bad. Horrible dreams, a bit spaced out, but I'll be OK,' Evie replied. 'Is there any news about Roddy?'

'He's been singing like the proverbial canary. He told us everything about the murders, in great detail. But after his lawyer arrived, he went quiet. It seems he wants to plead not guilty. He insists on having his day in court.'

'Yeah, I thought he'd want to do that. He'll want to

grandstand, to explain his theory that he's saved the island from tourists. He wants maximum coverage and publicity.'

'I'm sure you're right.'

'Will Fran and I have to testify?'

'Probably. But it won't be for quite a while yet, it can take anything from six months to a year before big cases like this come to court. So try not to worry about it, or think about it too much. OK, are you ready to begin with your statement?'

'Yes, fine.'

'We're going to do a video statement if that's OK with you?'

'Fine.'

Evie was able to speak clearly and dispassionately about the events of the previous day. She was a little distracted when she heard Fran's mobile phone ringing, and saw, through the window, that Fran had gone out into the garden to take the call. She was pacing up and down the tiny patch of grass, speaking earnestly. Probably the parents, Evie thought. They must have been following the case in the news.

Soon the interview was over. Sergeant Reid shook their hands and thanked them warmly for their help. He promised to keep them updated on any developments, and then the two officers were gone.

'Phew! It's over!' said Fran.

Evie let out a long breath. 'For now. Until it goes to court. Apparently he's intending to plead not guilty.'

'That's crazy. No way they'll find him innocent.'

'I'm not sure he even wants that. He just wants to have his moment in the spotlight.'

Fran nodded. 'Look,' she said, 'Let's forget about it all. Do you know what I fancy doing tonight?'

'Go on.'

'Getting a bottle of wine and a couple of glasses and walking up to that viewpoint again, Temptation Hill, and watching the sunset over Skye.'

'Great idea! The sun sets at about nine o clock, doesn't it? Shall we eat first?'

***

The sunset was magnificent and vast over the dark mountains. The scattering of cirrus clouds absorbed the sun's dying rays, glowing first a fiery orange, then slowly turning to crimson, then purple, then fading into the indigo sky as the first stars appeared. They clinked their glasses and drank their wine in companionable silence for a long while.

'Oh, by the way, who was that on the phone earlier on?' asked Evie, as the light began to fade and they packed up the glasses to head back. 'I saw you talking outside and you looked so serious.'

'Oh,' said Fran, giving Evie a considering look. 'Um... it was... actually it was Jake.'

'Jake? Why was he ringing you?'

'He wanted to make sure you were OK. He heard about the arrest.'

'What did you tell him?'

'Well, I told him quite a bit actually. How you almost got killed. Twice. How we helped catch the killer.'

'Oh, right.' Evie tried to imagine the conversation. Fran had always had an easy, jokey relationship with Jake, who she genuinely liked. In turn, he poked fun at Fran's London lifestyle and southern ways. That was their thing, sparring and mocking, but with affection. But how would such a serious conversation have played out? She couldn't see it.

'What did he say?' she asked.

'He was gobsmacked. Terrified for you, really upset.'

'Was he?'

'Yes, of course, you loon. He still loves you.'

'I'm not sure. He's got a new...'

'Evie, don't be thick. He still loves you. And I think you love him too. Am I right?'

Evie sighed. 'Yes,' she admitted.

'Well, then,' said Fran, with a hint of satisfaction. 'Don't write anything off. Things might still work out.' She put out a hand to pull Evie off the bench. 'Come on, let's get back to the cottage before it's too dark.'

They spent a quiet evening watching an old Richard Curtis romantic comedy on TV, snuggled together on the sofa with the tartan throws around their knees and a bowl of crisps on their lap. They'd both seen the film a couple of times before, but it was safe and comfortable, and allowed them to escape into a world where good things happen to good people, and everything turns out right in the end.

CHAPTER SEVENTEEN: THE BEACH

Evie yawned and padded down the narrow stairs to the kitchen, rubbing the sleep from her eyes.

'Morning! Any nightmares last night?' she asked Fran.

'No, I actually slept quite well, amazingly. What about you?'

'Same here. I feel almost normal today. I'll put the kettle on. Have you been up long?'

'No, only about ten minutes.'

The sisters drank their tea, then made bacon sandwiches. Fran went up to take a shower while Evie stacked the dishwasher.

There was a loud knock at the door. Evie's instant reaction was to panic; any unexpected noise sent her nervous system into flight mode, as her brain pumped extra blood and oxygen to her muscles, and adrenaline sharpened her senses. Heart racing, she went into the hallway. She could see a dark shape the other side of the opaque glass in the door panel.

'Fran!' called Evie, in an urgent whisper, 'there's someone at the door!'

Fran appeared at the top of the stairs with a towel wrapped around her body.

'Don't open it. Better check who it is. It might be a reporter.'

Evie approached the door, cautiously. 'Who is it?' she called.

'It's me, Jake.'

Evie did a double-take. It couldn't be Jake! He was at home

in Yorkshire. Wasn't he?

'Jake? Is that really you?'

'Yes of course it's me. You can open the door.'

Evie was suddenly conscious of her pyjamas, baggy at the knees and elbows, her unwashed hair, her unbrushed teeth. She opened the door and they stared at each other for a long moment, neither moving.

'Can I come in?' asked Jake, at last.

'Oh, yes, of course,' said Evie, stepping aside to let him enter. 'What are you doing here?'

'I had to see you,' said Jake. 'I had to check with my own eyes, make sure you're really OK. God, I'm so glad to see you!'

'How did you get here?'

'I drove. I set off at nine last night.'

'Bloody hell, you must be knackered! Come into the kitchen. Do you want a coffee? Or tea?'

Evie turned blindly to the kitchen counter, flustered and confused. She couldn't look at him; it hurt too much. With her back to him, busying herself with the kettle, she could sense him there, so strong, so dependable, so solid. She'd tried to distance herself from him, but now here he was, a massive presence in the tiny kitchen, and suddenly her own body felt alive, tingly, extra sensitive, all her senses heightened.

'Evie, stop fiddling. Come and sit down,' said Jake.

Reluctantly she turned and sat at the table facing him. She looked into his eyes, the clear mid-brown irises rimmed with chocolate brown, tired now, behind the round wire-framed glasses. He looked older than she remembered; there were new lines around his eyes and mouth. The stubble on his chin was more pronounced than usual, and Evie itched to touch it, to feel the prickly hairs springing back under her fingers. She gave herself a mental shake. You don't know how this is going to go, she warned herself. Don't get your hopes up.

'We've not talked properly since you moved out. I want to have an honest talk, get everything out into the open. Can we do that?'

Evie was about to answer when Fran burst into the kitchen, fully dressed and smelling of fragrant apple shower gel.

'Jake!' she cried, 'What the hell? You must have been driving all night!'

'Had to come,' said Jake, getting up from his chair and enveloping Fran in a bear hug.

They clung to each other and rocked back and forth, and Evie felt a rare stab of jealousy towards her sister. They're so easy together! So natural. He didn't hug me. He hasn't touched me. Why not? Uncertainty gnawed at her again. What had he come to say to her? Maybe he wanted a divorce?

Fran pushed Jake away gently and took the situation in hand. 'Right,' she said, 'You two need to talk, but Jake, you look like shit. Go and crash out on my bed for a couple of hours. Evie, you don't look much better. Get yourself into the shower. You can talk the arses off each other when you look human again.'

'God, you're still a bossy cow, aren't you?' smiled Jake, and he followed Fran up the stairs, leaving Evie gazing at his retreating back

**

Four hours later, Fran shooed them out of the cottage with a bag of ham rolls and orders not to come back too soon. They wandered down the road, side by side, not speaking, not touching. Evie sneaked little glances at him, but his expression was hard to read. They soon arrived at the pebble beach which overlooked the sound of Raasay. Evie slowed down.

'We saw an otter here on... God, it was only two days ago. Thursday. Feels like weeks ago.'

'Let's sit,' said Jake, lowering himself onto the bank.

Oh God, thought Evie, as she sat down beside him. This is it. Moment of truth. She simultaneously longed for and dreaded this conversation. But Jake surprised her by asking about the murders.

'Fran told me a bit about what happened. But what made you go off alone with that man? Didn't you think it could be dangerous?'

Evie shrugged. 'No, not really. He'd been with us every day of the week of the painting holiday, and he was always really charming - quiet, helpful, a bit innocent, unworldly. We both trusted him. And I was almost sure the killer was this other man, Arthur Ross. He'd threatened me at the hotel, told me to watch myself or an accident might happen.'

'Right, I see.' Jake scratched his chin before asking: 'Did you fancy this Roddy guy?'

Evie paused. It seemed crazy now, in retrospect, but... 'Total honesty? I was trying to make myself like him. I was trying to imagine a life without you. You'd moved on, so I kind of... made myself fancy him, just a bit. He reminded me of you, in a way. Solid and dependable – at least, that's the image he projected. He had us all fooled.'

'Shit, really? But Evie,' he looked her in the eyes, his gaze steady and earnest, 'I hadn't moved on. I didn't have a new girlfriend.'

'But Becca told me...'

'Becca lied. And I've had a right go at her for that. Silly cow.'

'Why would she lie?'

'You must know how jealous she is of you?'

'Is she?'

'You didn't realise? Yes, she's jealous. You know, you're good at your job, people like you – and then you go and marry her cousin. She said she felt you were stealing me away from her.

And her own marriage isn't working out that great, so I think she couldn't help trying to ruin ours.'

'So you never went to dinner at Becca's with a new girlfriend?'

'There's absolutely no new girlfriend. No-one.'

Evie nodded slowly. 'All this time, I thought… God, that's why I got the flat. That's why I wrote that email to you, instead of picking up the phone. I was really hurt.'

'And I didn't know you thought that. I thought you'd just turned against me, or that your parents had poisoned your feelings against me. But, going back to the murders, how did you get away from the guy? Fran said you were alone with him on top of a mountain somewhere.'

'I pepper sprayed him and kicked him in the balls.'

'Did you? Fucking good job! But then he came back to have another go. How did he know where to find you?'

'I'm guessing he waited outside the police station. We were there for hours. And he must have seen us getting on the police boat and crossing over to Raasay.'

'And you were waiting for him?'

'Yes, I'd had another vision that he was getting off the ferry.' She glanced up at him. Usually he hated any mention of premonitions, visions, flashes, and his scepticism would show in his pursed lips and narrowed eyes, but today he just looked thoughtful. 'So we went to the distillery to be around people. He found us there.'

'What happened at the distillery?'

'It was weird. He came up to us all smiling and charming and normal – then he said he didn't know which one of us to kill. He just changed in an instant. It was chilling. Fran and I pushed the table into his midriff and he dropped the knife. I picked it up but I was trembling so much I couldn't use it. He was coming closer and closer, and he knew I couldn't do it… Then the distillery men came and tackled him. I don't know what would have happened if they hadn't come at that moment.'

'That's twice you got the better of him, though. You should be really proud, you and Fran. You caught a serial killer.'

They were silent for a long moment, their eyes glued to the sea and the misty mountains on the other side of the sound.

'So there was no new girlfriend?' Evie said at last.

'No.'

'But why didn't you talk to me after I moved out? You never phoned, you never came to see me. What was I supposed to think?'

'I overreacted when you went to Glasgow, I suppose. I wanted to hit back at you, so I asked you to go to your parents' place. I never thought it'd be for more than a week or so. But then I was too stubborn to make the first move, and after that you found yourself a flat and I just assumed you didn't want me any more. You said you wanted to sell the house. I assumed it was over.'

'Bloody Becca! But we've got to talk about Glasgow. I was wrong to...'

'It's OK, I get it, I overreacted. It's my fault.' Jake interrupted.

'No, listen. I need you to really understand how important it was to me. It wasn't for nothing. I really believed that I had a sort of psychic ability to make things work out for my benefit, and that sometimes other people would get hurt as a result. You know that. I believed it. And it made me lose all my confidence and stop enjoying the house, and stop enjoying our relationship in a way – I thought I'd got you unfairly by making your girlfriend's mum get cancer.' She saw the look of incredulity on Jakes face. 'I know it sounds crazy now, but that's what I believed. Things always worked in my favour. I had to find out if that was true or not, so that's why I went to Glasgow to do the tests. And they showed that I can get premonitions, but I can't change things. It was such good news, such a relief. It was the right thing to do, going to do the tests. But I should have told you, convinced you. I shouldn't have lied to you.'

'Maybe. I would've been annoyed at you going, I suppose, even if you'd told me.' Jake turned his gaze from the sea to look straight into her eyes. 'Evie, will you come back? Will you give us another chance?'

This was everything that Evie wanted to hear, but still she hesitated. There was something else that needed to be addressed.

'Jake, I love you. But I can't come back unless one thing changes; it'll always come between us.' She took a deep breath. 'Jake, I know you hate that I have premonitions. It makes you uncomfortable. You prefer to think they're not real. It goes against your down-to-earth, pragmatic life-view. That's why I never really talked about them to you. But, Jake, they are real. They are important. And they are a part of me. If you can't accept the premonitions, that means you don't really fully accept me.'

'Fair point.' He nodded. 'I didn't like it when you talked about premonitions. I thought it was flaky and it scared me stiff to think you were flaky. But I've got to start believing them now, haven't I? You saw a murder scene and it played out exactly as you saw it, according to Fran. You saw that man getting off a ferry and that's exactly what he did. So, yes, I'm going to try hard to understand them, not to pooh-pooh them. I promise. So will you come back?'

Evie let a beat go, then she smiled. 'Of course I will.'

At last Jake made a move. He put his arm round her shoulders as they sat side by side, and pulled her towards him. He kissed the top of her head. She let her head fall onto his shoulder and breathed in his wonderful familiar smell – part motor oil, part warm skin, and sighed.

Jake lifted her left hand and rubbed his thumb along her third finger. 'Still wearing your wedding ring, then?'

Evie looked down at her finger. 'Of course!'

They sat gazing out over the water, perfectly content, for ten or twenty minutes, listening to the gentle dragging and rolling sounds of the sea playing with the pebbles on the shoreline. There were no otters, no dolphins or basking sharks, just the usual wading birds – turnstones and sandpipers - scuttling busily here and there and rootling in the seaweed for insects and molluscs.

To Evie, the moment could not have been more idyllic. She was home.

***

Fran smiled to herself when she looked out the window and saw the couple returning to the cottage, hand in hand, heads down, laughing and chatting. About bloody time, she thought. She opened the door for them, but didn't comment, just gave Evie a little surreptitious wink as she hung her jacket on the hook.

'I've been to the shop,' she said. 'I got us a couple of steak pies again for dinner later. Hope you're hungry!'

'Starving!' said Jake.

When they entered the kitchen Evie saw a pile of newspapers on the table. 'What did you get these for?' she asked, eyeing the papers nervously.

'Well, I thought we'd better have a look. I haven't read them all, but you know yesterday, Evie, there was nothing much in the papers, it just said they'd caught the killer, and how old he was, and that he was a Skye local. Well today the press have got hold of the whole story, somehow. The anti-tourism angle. And it's going absolutely viral. I think it's going to be a huge big deal. The journalists might be on our trail for interviews soon.'

'Does it mention us already?'

'I don't think so. Not really. One paper says Roddy

McAllister was caught attempting to murder two English tourists at the Raasay distillery. It doesn't name us. But I expect they'll work it out soon.'

'Someone at the distillery must have spoken to the press, I guess. One of the workers, maybe, or the old couple. We'd better sit down and read them all, then.'

Fran had bought a copy of each paper the little shop stocked: the Daily Telegraph, the Scotsman, the Daily Record, the Daily Mail and the Press and Journal. Evie spread the papers out, looking at the headlines and photos on each cover. She stared at the cover of the Telegraph, one of Britain's least sensational broadsheets. The bold headline was 'Anti-tourism Vigilante Kills Five' and the photo showed Roddy in his mountain guide gear, looking handsome and capable. The Daily Record headline was 'Skye Tourist Killer Shock' in huge block capitals, next to a photo of the Old Man of Storr. The Daily Mail headline screamed 'Tourist Slaughter on Popular Island' and showed composite photos of the five victims. Evie's fingers brushed the little photo of Kayleigh, and suddenly the full horror of Kayleigh's death hit her with force. Such a beautiful, quirky girl, so young and full of potential, such a terrible way to die. The bastard, fucking, fucking bastard. I hope he rots in prison for the rest of his life.

Fran plonked three glasses of beer on the table, breaking Evie's furious thoughts, and the three of them sat down to read.

All the papers had somehow got the gist of the story correct, that a lone killer had been targeting tourists in a bid to limit their numbers on the Isle of Skye. They described each killing again - the tabloids revelling in lurid detail - and linked the killings to the recent anti-tourism protests on the island. The more serious papers then went on to describe the growing trend of tourism-phobia and the local protests in other countries, especially in Spain, Greece and Italy. The inside pages devoted space to the widely divergent views of angry locals and tourism industry workers.

'Christ,' said Jake, looking at his phone, 'it's all over the internet. YouTube, Buzzfeed, Facebook, X... People are sharing their stories and new ones are popping up all the time, it's crazy.'

'What's the vibe? Are people horrified, or kind of sympathetic?' asked Fran.

'A bit of both really, but I'd say the majority are kind of saying 'we've had enough, it was only a matter of time.' There's a whole bunch of people from Skye who talk about what upsets them. And I must admit, some of this would drive me mad, too.'

'Give us some examples,' said Evie.

'This one bloke here, his mother died because she had a heart attack and the ambulance couldn't get to the house because of badly parked cars. Another bloke talks about camper vans emptying their chemical toilets into the rivers. Lots of people complain about poo and toilet paper being left on the footpaths, or people leaving their waste lying around after picnics. Literally dozens of comments about people not knowing how to drive properly on narrow roads. A woman here couldn't get out of her house 'cos a car parked blocking her driveway...'

'What about counter arguments? Anyone sticking up for the tourists?'

'Yeah, a couple. There's a comment here about a quarter of the population of Skye working in the tourism sector, that it's the lifeblood of the island, and what would happen to the island if that stopped. And some people are starting to talk about solutions, like a tourism tax, or a toll on the Skye Bridge, or banning Airbnbs, like they did in Barcelona.'

Evie wondered if Roddy had access to a phone or to newspapers in his cell. She thought probably not. But if he did, he would be delighted by the coverage his murders had received, and by the upswell of anti-tourist indignation that had been stirred up. The bastard was probably smirking, believing himself to be a local hero.

'Oh, look,' said Fran, a worried frown on her face. 'The Daily Record talks about us. It says '*the avenging angel of over-tourism narrowly failed in his attempt to kill two young female visitors on the isle of Raasay on Thursday. He was apprehended by distillery workers at the Raasay distillery, brandishing a knife and shouting death threats to tourists.*"

'Any comment from the police?' asked Jake.

'Just a comment from some Chief Inspector or something, saying again that this is a one-off, and that people shouldn't be put off coming to Skye. This story's going to run and run,' said Fran. 'It won't take the journalists long to work out who we are and where we're staying. I think we should pack up and leave tomorrow.'

'Yes, I suppose you're right,' said Evie, reluctantly. 'What d'you think, Jake? Can you bear another long drive back south?'

'Yeah, of course. And we don't have to go all the way; we could stop overnight in the Borders somewhere.'

'Right,' said Evie. 'That's decided. I'll phone the police and tell them we're going.'

Jake looked at his phone. 'The first ferry off the island is at quarter to eight tomorrow. Shall we go for that one?'

'OK,' said Fran. 'I'll put the pies in the oven, then we can start packing.'

***

The spell of good weather broke the next morning, and they woke up to dull, sunless skies. The air felt heavy and the mountains had disappeared under a veil of low, grey cloud. Rain threatened. Despite the weather, Evie was sad to leave the cottage. It had been a refuge of peace, quiet and simplicity, and now they were heading back to their real lives. There would be her parents' endless questions and shocked reactions to manage, plus her colleagues' curiosity about a Skye holiday coinciding with a spate of murders. She had to face Becca, too, and figure out a way to work closely with a girl who was not her biggest fan. She had to manage her own emotions too; she was still in a state of heightened anxiety, jumping at the slightest unexpected noise, and finding her heart racing for no apparent reason. But now things were different. She had Jake by her side, and knew she could face all these challenges with greater equanimity.

The previous evening had been wonderful. She and Jake had talked for hours, agreeing she should give up the lease on the Wakefield flat as soon as it was possible. Jake would hire a van the following week and they would bring back her furniture, redirect her mail, contact the utility companies, and give the place a quick clean. Then they would go straight back to living together in the lovely stone-built house in Newmillerdam. All Evie's negative feelings about the house had melted away, and she could hardly wait to see it again. She longed to be back in the garden, pulling up weeds, or strolling around the country park kicking up autumn leaves, or just sitting on the sofa watching the TV with Jake by her side. All that she had lost was now thrillingly within reach again. She'd been given a second chance, and she was determined to appreciate every aspect of it. The prospect of even the most banal activities, like repainting the spare bedroom, or cooking dinner after a long day at work, now seemed imbued with a kind of magic, and she was not going to take a single second of it for granted. That night they had made love with such tenderness, such relief, that it had made them both cry.

Now, Evie locked the cottage door and dropped the keys off with the shopkeeper at the little general store. She waved goodbye, then got into the car beside Jake, and they followed Fran's car down to the harbour, queuing up for the ferry with five or six other vehicles. As the vessel approached across the water, they could just make out three white vans on the car deck. And when the ferry docked, and the vans began to move off, they saw the unmistakable white spheres attached to the roofs. Satellite dishes! News vans! With a feeling of satisfaction and relief, they watched the news vans drive past their cars and head on up the hill. Then they boarded the ferry and were on their way. They'd escaped.

Just under an hour later the two cars were once more on the narrow arc of the Skye bridge, heading towards the mainland. The mist-shrouded mass of the Black Cuillin mountains receded slowly from view behind them. Evie felt a huge wave of relief flood her body.

The nightmare was over.

C HAPTER EIGHTEEN: HOME

Eight months later

'What about Laura?'

'Nah, I went to school with a Laura. She was a pain in the arse.'

'Lauren then?'

'Yeah, that's nicer. Add it to the list.'

'I like Chloe and Zoe. Mia too.'

'Hmm, not sure. I prefer really old-fashioned, plain names like Anna and Louise.'

'Don't you want a name that's a bit different?'

'No, not really. What was your grandmother's name?'

'Nelly.'

'I actually quite like that! We can add it to the list.'

Evie was lying across the sofa in her oversize pyjamas, with her feet on Jake's lap. He was kneading her feet and gently massaging her swollen ankles. Evie's hand rested lightly on her bump, capturing the delicate rippling and pushing sensations of the baby as it moved inside her.

'Are you sure it's a girl?' Jake asked.

'Yes, well, about ninety percent anyway.'

It was a cold Sunday morning in April. The new log burner was radiating a pleasant heat throughout the room, and the Spotify Chill Mix playlist that Jake had created added to the indolent, cosy atmosphere. Jake's parents were coming over for lunch later, but the goulash had been prepared the previous evening. Jake's thumbs pressed gently into the soles of Evie's feet, and she groaned with pleasure.

'God, that feels so relaxing,' she said. 'I could fall asleep.'

'Are you not worried about the trial coming up?' asked Jake. 'You seem really calm about it.'

Evie reached forward to lay the pen and paper on the coffee table, then leant back again and looked at Jake, her head on one side and her chin supported in the palm of one hand.

'I'm not worried, 'cos I don't think there's going to be a trial,' she said.

'Oh! What makes you say that? A vision?'

'No, more a kind of sense of certainty. I know I'm not going to have to give evidence.'

'Hmm.' Jake wrinkled his brow in concentration and ran a hand through the bristles on his chin. 'Well, let's try and figure out what that means. Do you think he's going to change his plea to guilty?'

'I'm hoping so. But I can't really see him doing that. It's not in his character. Unless he's had a massive crisis of conscience, or found religion, or something.'

'Or maybe one of the inmates is going to attack him in jail? I could imagine that might happen with serial killers. They must be targets for the hard men. Is he being kept in solitary?'

'I don't know.'

'Or maybe he's going to commit suicide.'

'I can't imagine that, either. He's not the type. He's totally convinced he's in the right.'

'There is another possibility,' said Jake, eyeing her cautiously. 'What if he's planning to escape?'

'Oh, God forbid. But no-one escapes from prison these days, do they? It's pretty much impossible. He's in the highest security prison, somewhere in Lanarkshire. And he's a loner. He doesn't have a network of criminals to break him out. I don't know what to think. Maybe he's ill, got cancer or something, and they're going to delay everything?'

'Who knows. But anyway, it's good you're not stressing out about it. We can just concentrate on little Lauren.'

'Little Nelly, you mean! Actually Grannie's real name was Ellen and they shortened it to Nelly. What do you think of Ellen?'

'That's nice! A definite contender.'

Jake lifted her feet from his lap and got up to put another log on the wood burner. Evie watched as he carefully chose the right log and gently opened the door of the stove to stop the smoke billowing out. I do love that man, she thought. She closed her eyes and let her head rest on the arm of the sofa. Within minutes she was asleep.

***

Two weeks later, Evie and Becca were poring over a set of photos and creating copy to update the Visit Leeds Facebook page, when her mobile phone rang. Annoyed to be distracted when she was on a roll at work, she answered with a touch of exasperation in her voice:

'Yeah, hello?'

'Mrs Carpenter?'

'Yes, that's me.' Evie recognised the gentle Highland accent immediately, and was at once alert.

'I have some bad news for you, I'm afraid,' said Sergeant Reid.

'Hold on a sec,' said Evie, 'I'll just go somewhere more private.'

She gestured 'sorry' across the table to Becca, and took her phone into one of the tiny offices along the corridor.

'OK, go ahead,' she said, closing the door behind her.

'It's concerning Roddy McAllister. I'm really sorry to tell you that he has escaped from prison and has not yet been apprehended.'

Somehow Evie was not surprised. She accepted the news quite calmly.

'But how on earth did he manage to escape?' she asked.

'It seems he pretended to be seriously ill. He was vomiting and convulsing apparently. I don't know how he managed to fool everyone. But they didn't restrain him. They put him on a stretcher to take him in the ambulance to the A&E department of the local hospital, a university hospital with low security. There were guards escorting him, of course, but he'd made some kind of homemade weapon, and he got away from them. We think he probably had an accomplice, someone to drive him away. I am deeply, deeply sorry that this has happened.'

'So you don't know where he is now?'

'I'm afraid not. But you could be in danger again. He knows where you work, doesn't he?'

'He won't come here.'

'You don't know that. He's already made two attempts on your life.'

'No, he won't come south. I just know. He's a Highlander. Skye is his lifeblood, his oxygen. He wouldn't survive in a city. He'd be a fish out of water. Believe me, he'll go back to Skye, I'm sure.'

'You seem very certain.'

'Yes, I feel like I understand the way he thinks, a bit. He has no interest in England. He had no real interest in me, he just wanted another victim. He won't come after me.'

'So, where do you think he'll go?'

Evie paused, considering. She concentrated, trying to summon a mental image of Roddy, on the run, hiding out. He knew every inch of the island: all the mountain paths, the hidden glens and abandoned settlements. She had an idea:

'He likes to think he's a modern-day Bonnie Prince Charlie or Robert the Bruce. Both of them hid in caves when they were being hunted. If I were you, I'd try all the caves on Skye first.'

Seargeant Reid sighed audibly. 'There are over two hundred caves on Skye, and thousands of metres of secret tunnels. That'll be a mammoth task. But you're right, we'll have to check them all.'

'And you could check the deserted crofts and chapels. Anywhere isolated, off the road.'

'And what do you think he'll do?'

Evie hesitated, reluctant to be so pessimistic, but then said bluntly: 'I think he'll start again. I think he'll look for his next victim.'

'Oh God.' He sighed again, heavily. 'Who will he go for? Any idea?'

'He said he wanted to get a camper van. I don't know if he meant he just wanted to damage the van, or to kill the people inside. That was next on his list.'

'OK, we'll put a watch on all the caravan parks.'

'You said he might have had help breaking out of prison,' said Evie. 'Do you think there are people on Skye who are helping him?'

'I think it's possible. He's got no money, no food, no clothes, no transport, no roof over his head. Someone must be helping him. We've been monitoring the internet, and there are some crackpots who see him as a kind of modern day hero. They could be keeping him hidden. We're checking the movements and phones of everyone we've become suspicious of.'

'You'll find him. I'm sure you will. He can't stay hidden for ever; it's impossible in the modern world with CCTV cameras everywhere and traceable phone records, isn't it? Even on a remote island like Skye.'

'We've got a big team together now, with reinforcements from stations all over the Highlands helping with the manhunt. We will find him. And if you get any of your strange visions, you be sure to let us know. Anything you see might be a vital clue, even the smallest little detail.'

'I will, of course.'

'But you take care of yourself, Mrs Carpenter. Keep safe.'

'I will. Thank you.'

'Oh, and by the way, have you still got that illegal can of pepper spray that we didn't charge you for possessing?'

Evie actually laughed. 'Yes, I think it's around, somewhere.'

'You find it. Keep it in you pocket. Goodbye now.'

'Bye.'

Evie cut the call, then immediately phoned Jake to tell him the news. He was horrified.

'I think you should stop work. Stay home. He knows you work for Visit Leeds. He could easily find you,' he panicked.

'He won't. I know he won't, Jake, don't worry. I'm not stopping work.'

'Well, I'm going to give you a lift to work and from work every day until he's caught again.'

'You don't have to…'

'No arguments! I won't get a moment's rest unless you let me do that. I've got to keep my two girls safe.'

Evie laughed. 'Well, OK then, if it makes you feel better. Now get back to changing the oil filters, or whatever you're doing. I need to phone Fran.'

'I'll be outside the door at five. Bye.'

'Bye.'

Evie cut the call and sat down on one of the office chairs. She closed her eyes and searched for clues. She tried to analyse how she was feeling. She wasn't scared. She was certain that he would not come for her. She could picture him now, already back in his beloved Hebridean mountains, zig-zagging up hidden deer tracks to find secluded, narrow glens, running through the heather like a latter-day Jacobean rebel, reddish hair streaming behind him, feet splashing through bogs and hand resting on his dagger. He would kill again. But it felt somehow... inevitable, preordained. Like seeing the lynx return to the Alps, the bear to the Pyrenees, the wildcat to the uplands of Scotland. A natural predator, the top of the food chain, was returning to his native kingdom.

And although she detested him for what he had done to Kayleigh and the others, and for everything that he had put her and Fran through, she admitted to herself that a tiny, tiny part of her was rejoicing in his freedom, in his unfettered joy at being back in his homeland.

Is there something wrong with me, she wondered. Why am I not horrified? Why am I not desperately scared for the poor unsuspecting tourists planning their summer trips to Skye? Is it because I'm safely hundreds of miles away? Because I can look at it dispassionately, as an outsider? She knew she had a dark side to her character; she had always felt a little thrill of awe and fascination when she watched weather disasters wreak havoc on the TV; a tornado destroying a Midwest town, a flood wiping out a riverside community, a wildfire devouring luxurious Californian villas. Awful, but at the same time gripping, enthralling. Nature fighting back, nature saying 'stop, enough is enough'.

And here was Roddy, saying again 'enough is enough.'

If she was honest with herself, she knew that a small, perverse, rebellious part of her was pleased.

EPILOGUE

'Christ, what did you put in my fucking backpack? It weighs a fucking ton!' said Charlie, pulling on the straps to try and shift the pack to a more comfortable position. His shoulders were aching and his boots were letting in water. This was not the camping trip he had envisaged. When Spencer had suggested this trip he had imagined there would be neatly partitioned pitches, a large pre-erected tent with separate sleeping areas, a clean shower block, and most importantly, a bar within walking distance full of local girls to chat up. But here they were at the very edge of existence, miles and miles from the nearest house, clambering over alternately rocky and boggy ground, headed for God knows where.

'You've got the food and drink. But hey, man, I've got the tent, so think yourself lucky. Anyway, it can't be far now,' said Spencer. 'You'll love it when you see it.'

'Bloody well hope so,' grumbled Charlie. 'This is the arse end of nowhere. I've no fucking idea why you brought us here.'

'You'll see. It's supposed to be the best beach on the island, better than the Caribbean even. Come on, man, where's your spirit of adventure? Wild camping! Just channel your inner Bear Grylls.'

'Bear Grylls can fuck right off,' Charlie complained. 'And Bear Grylls had a whole fucking TV crew with him. Are you sure we're even on the right track? I don't trust your map-reading skills.'

'Jesus, don't be such a misery. There was only one path. I looked it up. The website said it was about three miles from where the road just ended. We must have done nearly three already.'

'And I don't think you should have parked the Audi in front of that gate. What if the farmer needs to get into the field?'

'For Gods sake, will you stop being such a fucking old woman! No-one lives around here, I haven't seen a single farm, have you? Come on. I reckon it's just over the next hill.'

Charlie sighed and trudged doggedly after his friend, silently cursing the slippery rocks and tangled heather that caught at his boots. Not for the first time, he wished he'd gone with his parents to New York. He could have been in a luxury hotel right now, with a spa, five star restaurant and king size bed. But at least it wasn't raining. It was actually quite warm for May.

The path continued to rise for a few hundred metres, then at the top of the next hill it descended steeply and they caught their first sight of the beach. It was incredible. The horse-shoe of sand was pure white and unmarked by a single footprint. The sea was a clear turquoise near the shore, blending to an azure blue as the water got deeper. Further along the shoreline creatures had hauled out onto flat rocks to bask in the sunshine. Were they seals? Or sealions? Charlie wasn't sure.

Spencer let out a whoop of enthusiasm and ran down the last few metres to the beach, his backpack bumping against the base of his spine. Then he threw off the pack, spread his arms out wide and turned in a slow circle. 'This is fucking amazing, isn't it?' he called to his friend.

'Yeah, I'll admit this is pretty cool,' said Charlie, coming more slowly down the grassy bank to join him. 'So what's the plan?'

'Let's get the tent up first. Then we'll get the drone out and do some filming. After that we'll build a decent fire and go skinny dipping.'

'You want to go swimming in that? In the nuddy? You must be off your fucking rocker. It'll freeze your bollocks off.'

'That's what we'll have built the fire for, thicko. We'll drink some vodka for Dutch courage, smoke a joint or two, then we'll swim. You'll get a real high when you come out of the water.'

The two boys began unpacking the groundsheet, canvas, pegs and poles.

'Are you sure this is above the high tide mark?' asked Charlie.

'Yeah, I reckon so. Hope the pegs hold in the sand, though. They don't seem very long.'

'Shouldn't we dig into the wetter sand? It'll be more solid.'

'Nah, it'll be fine. It's not windy.'

Neither boy looked up. If they had, they might have seen a lone figure standing on the top of the grassy bank. The man watched as the boys struggled to pitch the tent. He crouched behind a rock as they flew their drone back and forth across the bay, shouting and waving for the camera and scaring the sealions into the water. He watched as they desecrated the pristine beach by arranging a circle of rocks on it, into which they dropped piles of driftwood for the fire. His fingers curled around his knife and his eyes narrowed as he saw the blond boy toss the empty vodka bottle carelessly behind him, where it smashed against a rock. His hand gripped the knife yet tighter as the other boy ran to the grass and dropped his pants to defecate, not bothering to cover his mess. Then he smiled grimly to himself as the fire took hold, and the two boys ripped off their t-shirts, hopping on one leg to pull off their jeans and underpants, and finally yelling and cursing as they felt the icy-cold seawater reach their groin area.

They're making it so easy, thought the man, his sharp, amber-coloured eyes narrowing against the low sun as he followed the boys' progress into deeper water. Different options presented themselves to him. He could slash the tent to ribbons and throw their clothes and boots into the fire. The boys would probably die a lingering death, clinging to each other for warmth when the temperature dropped to around three degrees that night. They would begin to shiver, then their breathing would become shallow, their heart rates would slow and their brains would become confused. They would fall into a coma, then their breathing would stop. All he had to do was wait. Then, when the morning light returned, he could simply arrange their frozen limbs with legs straight and arms folded across their chests. Or it might be fun to dispose of their clothes and hunt the naked boys as they stumbled blindly, barefoot, and in the dark, over the moorland towards their car, only to find the tyres slashed. Or he could simply walk down to the beach and just stand there, on the shoreline, his knife glinting in the evening sunshine, and wait for the boys to emerge.

The boys spluttered, yelled and laughed as they wrestled in the waves and dived under the water to pull the legs out from under each other. As the sun began to sink towards the horizon and the sky grew darker, they had eyes only on the other's body, searching for the best wrestling hold. The did not see the dark figure approach the campfire. They did not notice the fire splutter and sparks rise as each item of clothing was fed into it. Their joyous shouts covered the ripping sound of the thick tent fabric being sliced again and again by a short Scottish dagger.

Charlie and Spencer - two privileged, thoughtless Cambridge undergraduates. Two young, naïve tourists, who had arrogantly assumed this magnificent island was their personal playground. So careless, so blindly trusting.

And soon to be so very, very dead.

Roddy kicked sand into the fire to extinguish the flames, zipped up his warm jacket, picked up the two sleeping bags and wandered slowly up to the top of the bank, where he could sit and wait for the coming tragedy to unfold. He watched the sky turn from blue to slate grey and the sea take on a deeper, indigo hue. He noticed black clouds building up in the distance, behind the islands of Rum, Canna and Eigg. He nodded to himself, satisfied.

Rain would come that night.

He fetched a piece of hard wood from his pocket and began to whittle.

ACKNOWLEDGEMENT

Enormous thanks go to my two early readers, Cathy Shahani and Christine Ferry, who suggested many plot improvements and spotted a couple of inconsistencies.

The job of proofreader is long and laborious, and I owe the greatest debt of gratitude to Sheila Carrodus, who corrected the many typos, spelling mistakes and grammar errors which inevitably creep in when you're on a writing roll. Sheila, you are a star!

Thanks to my husband Gordon, who frequently traipsed upstairs to help me with fiddly computer bits - and didn't complain *too* much.

Thanks to my son James, who helped with cover design and more fiddly bits beyond my ken, like HTML.

Thanks to my daughter Annie, for being so encouraging and supportive.

And finally, thanks to you, reader, for reading this book!

ABOUT THE AUTHOR

Kate Leonard

Kate Leonard was born and raised in Wakefield, West Yorkshire. She studied languages at Surrey University and worked first as a tour operator, then as a language teacher.
She moved to France in 1996 with her husband and two children, and currently lives in a village near Grenoble in the French Alps.

BOOKS BY THIS AUTHOR

Fall Line

"Oh yes, I remember the murder game" he said. "I still play it sometimes."

When Ellie is invited by best friend Kat to join a ski party in a remote Swiss resort, her first instinct is to say no. She doesn't like Kat's new bunch of friends, especially dark, brooding boyfriend Neil.

Reluctantly she agrees and is gradually drawn into the strange, tense circle. Each night, huddled round the fire in the isolated chalet, they play the murder game, taking turns to imagine the most gruesome, twisted way to kill someone in a ski resort.

Many years later, an unexpected invitation arrives. A reunion is planned in the same remote spot. Once again Kat and Ellie find themselves thrown together with the enigmatic group. They are all mature adults now, surely – aren't they?

But Kat has been keeping secrets from Ellie. What really happened on the penultimate day of the holiday all those years ago?

Tensions mount in the chalet. The weather begins to close in and the snow falls steadily. Then, one by one, the guests start to disappear.

Could one of them be carrying out the murders for real?

The Jetty

'Do you remember that old house we used to play in? The one we called the Scooby-Doo house? I think we saw a murder there!'

When Jenny's childhood friend turns up out of the blue, claiming that they witnessed a murder when they were just ten years old, she initially dismisses it as nonsense. You wouldn't forget a thing like that!

But Claire is persuasive, and Jenny reluctantly agrees to help find out if something really did happen on that summer day in the grounds of the decaying country house.

But the more time she spends with Claire, the more uneasy she becomes. How well does she really know her former friend? What has happened to her in those missing years? Is she obsessed, delusional? Jenny finds herself torn between a nostalgic loyalty to the girl she used to idolise, and a growing suspicion that Claire is mentally unstable.

As she gets sucked deeper and deeper into the mystery, cracks in her marriage appear and Jenny's comfortable suburban life begins to spin out of control.

But what if Claire isn't crazy? What if a murder really was committed on that long-ago day?

And by hunting the truth, could the two women find themselves instead becoming the hunted?

One Little Push

Erin is staring down fifty. On the surface she has everything - a supportive husband, good job, nice house - but more and more she finds herself consumed by mid-life rage. Is this all there is? Is this really the life she signed up for? The clock is ticking and she fizzes with frustration.

Her husband is bewildered, hurt, unable to help, and so Erin looks for answers in the past. Her thoughts return again and again to her teenage years when she joined a youth club with best friend Laura, a time of intense friendships, excitement and wonder. What became of those people?

But Erin's memories are flawed. She chooses to forget the cracks that appeared in the group when an enigmatic new member arrived, splintering it into rival factions. She prefers not to think about the bleak and ill-advised hiking trip to Malham Cove, when bitter arguments broke out as the hill fog descended. She has blocked out the horrific accident which saw one of them plunge hundreds of feet to their death from the treacherous cliff top.

But there's one person who never believed it was an accident.

And Erin's journey into the past triggers a deadly plan for revenge.

Printed in Dunstable, United Kingdom